"Must be nice to be a Boone." Kylee smiled.

Fisher nodded. "It is. I'm lucky."

She nodded, immediately caught up in the pull of his green eyes. The more time they spent together, the stronger it became. Especially when they were alone, like they were now. She wanted to go to him...but she couldn't move.

He did.

His hands settled on her shoulders and his thumbs trailed the ridges of her collarbones. How could such a light caress make her breathless? How could such a big man look at her with such tenderness?

"Kylee," he murmured.

"Fisher," she said, running her hands up his arms to grip his shoulders. The cotton of his shirt did little to cover the expanse of his shoulders. He was a strong man, a man who could be considered dangerous. But she knew the only danger he posed was to her heart.

Dear Reader,

Welcome back to Stonewall Crossing!

Small Texas towns are magical places. From town squares to main streets, the traditions and character of a place define the people—and vice versa. But there are drawbacks: everyone knows everyone else's business. So it can be incredibly hard for someone looking for a place to fade into the background or disappear altogether.

Kylee James's life has taught her one thing: don't trust anyone. Except maybe her twelve-year-old brother Shawn. From foster homes to living on the streets of Las Vegas, Kylee has done the best she could by her little brother. Including leaving Las Vegas for Stonewall Crossing.

Fisher Boone is a nice guy. The funny one. A good friend. (I'd love to play some pool with him.) But he's never had much luck with the ladies—not that he's ever minded much. Until Kylee James arrives in town. There's something fun about writing a big, manly man who falls in love for the first time. Fisher has a heart of gold; he's a giver and a protector. So having him both want to woo and protect this skittish, wary woman is hard work. But, as you'll see, Fisher isn't a quitter. Which is good news for Kylee.

I've become very attached to the Boone family and their work at the Veterinarian Teaching Hospital and their ranch. And, like before, there are plenty of animal adventures to keep all the Boone brothers busy. One of my favorite things about this book is the relationship between two of the brothers. You'll have to figure out which two I'm talking about and let me know what you think.

Happy reading!

Sasha Summers

COURTED BY THE COWBOY

—

SASHA SUMMERS

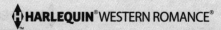
HARLEQUIN®WESTERN ROMANCE®

Recycling programs
for this product may
not exist in your area.

ISBN-13: 978-0-373-75723-7

Courted by the Cowboy

Printed in U.S.A.

www.Harlequin.com

Sasha Summers grew up surrounded by books. Her passions have always been storytelling, romance and travel. Whether it's an easy-on-the-eyes cowboy or a hero of truly mythic proportions, Sasha falls a little in love with each and every one of her heroes. She frequently gets lost with her characters in the worlds she creates, forgetting those everyday tasks like laundry and dishes. Luckily, her four brilliant children and hero-inspiring hubby are super understanding and helpful.

Books by Sasha Summers

Harlequin American Romance

The Boones of Texas

A Cowboy's Christmas Reunion
Twins for the Rebel Cowboy

Harlequin Blaze

Seducing the Best Man

All backlist available in ebook format.

Visit the Author Profile page at Harlequin.com for more titles.

Dedicated to my beloved friend Marilyn Tucker.

I miss your grammatical genius, your sparkling wit,
your wonderful hugs and your laughter.
Thank you for being a wonderful critique partner
and an even better friend.

Chapter One

Kylee glanced up as the door to Shots opened. Her pulse leaped and her legs tightened, ready to run. Ice-cold fear engulfed her, twisting her insides and making her lungs ache. An older gentleman shuffled in, tipping his well-worn cowboy hat in greeting before heading to the poker game taking place in the back corner. He was one of Cutter's friends, someone she'd seen before. Her nod was stiff, but her grip on the counter eased. She pulled in a deep breath, then blew it out, steadying herself. *We're safe.* At least she didn't freeze up anymore—or duck behind the counter. She was making progress.

The old man made his way across the scarred wooden floor to the group of men hunched over their beers and several decks of cards. A chorus of rough and creaky greetings welcomed the newcomer as he pulled a chair back to join them. *Nothing to fear there.* She took a deep breath, a slight smile on her lips.

Three wonderfully uneventful weeks had passed since she and her little brother, Shawn, arrived in Stonewall Crossing. Each day she woke up anticipating the worst. And each night she went to bed happy to be wrong. If Jesse or one of his low-life *associates* really wanted to find her, they would have by now. Her gaze wandered to the door again.

As if thinking about Jesse would somehow make him appear. That was ridiculous. She tossed her rag onto the bar and rubbed vigorously. She was sick and tired of jumping at her own shadow.

"You look ready to bolt." The voice startled her so much she dropped the rag. And jumped a good foot into the air.

"Dr. Boone." She pressed a hand to her chest as she stared at the man leaning against the end of the bar.

"I didn't mean to sneak up on you." He added, "And it's Fisher, Kylee. Only my patients get to call me Dr. Boone."

The thudding of her heart still echoed in her ears. "Your patients? As in, the dogs and cats?"

"I speak fluent dog and cat. It's a vet thing." He nodded, not cracking a smile. "My bird's a little rusty, though."

She pressed her lips together, fighting a smile. "When did you get here?"

Fisher stooped, picking up the rag and handing it to her. "I followed Ol' Pete in."

When she was having a minor panic attack. She nodded, working hard to pull herself together. The obvious concern on Fisher's face surprised her. She didn't like it. No one had ever worried over her. She didn't need anyone to start now. "Beer?" she asked.

"Sounds good." He was watching her—a little too closely for her liking.

She kept her eyes on his beer as she popped the top off a longneck and slid it across the counter toward him. "Good day, Doc?" she asked. Small talk was always a good distraction.

"No complaints." He shrugged. "You?"

"Just starting," she returned, flipping the switch that powered the wall of fluorescent beer and pool signs. The colored lights brightened the room and her mood.

The door opened to three women, chatting animatedly.

"Hey, Kylee." Janet was the only one Kylee knew by name. "Looks like we beat the rush."

"Can we have a round of beers?" one of the women asked, commandeering a table in front of the picture window that overlooked part of Stonewall Crossing's Main Street. "Bottles," she added.

"Please and thank you, Kylee." Janet winked.

Kylee was already popping the tops and putting them up on the counter.

Janet turned to Fisher. "Hey, Fisher, how's it going?"

From the way Janet got all giggly over Fisher's easy grin, it was clear Janet thought he was cute. And maybe he *did* have a nice grin, but that didn't amount to much. Kylee wasn't sure what to make of the hulking veterinarian. He was a little too tall and a little too broad. And he was nice—too nice. It made her nervous.

"Saving the world, one shih tzu at a time." Fisher saluted Janet with his beer.

"If I was single, Fisher Boone, I'd say you were the perfect man." She shook her head, laughing. "All big and muscle-y *and* a tender heart."

"That's me—a lover not a fighter."

Janet laughed. "You're adorable."

"I work hard at it," Fisher shot back.

Kylee glanced at Fisher, amused in spite of herself. He bobbed his eyebrows at her, trying to include her in the joke. So he had a pleasant grin. And a sense of humor. But something about him set off warning bells. She ignored

Fisher and said, "Janet, can you let your friend know we finally got that hard apple stuff she wanted to try."

"My friend?" Janet asked.

Kylee nodded. "From last week?"

"Oh, *that* one." Janet rolled her eyes. "You mean Winnie."

Kylee shrugged. The only thing she remembered about the woman was the ass chewing she got for not having some hard cider drink. When Kylee ordered new stock, she made sure to get some. Cutter told her to make customers happy, plain and simple. She wasn't about to argue with the man who'd turned her life around—even if the customer in question was a witch.

"She's not really a friend. But she's not exactly the type you want to make an enemy. When she wants to go out for a drink, you go." Janet took the beers and headed back to the table. "But I'll tell her."

"Janet speaks the truth." Fisher chuckled. "Beware Winnie Michaels."

Kylee wiped out a few glasses, getting ready for the regular after-work crowd. "Anyone else I should beware of?" She glanced at him again, trying not to let the weight of his steady green eyes bother her.

The corner of his eyes crinkled as he smiled. That was another thing. He smiled a lot. Maybe too much.

"I'll let you know," he offered. "Got plans for the weekend?"

She shook her head once. She and Shawn were planning on painting their tiny apartment—Cutter was letting them rent the addition at the back of the bar until they found a "more suitable place." As far as she and Shawn were concerned, it was perfectly suitable.

She did need to talk to Cutter about finding a resale

shop. She wanted to get some bicycles so she and Shawn could explore. But none of that was any of Fisher's business so she didn't say a word.

"All that?" He set his beer on the counter. "Damn, Kylee. Sounds like you'll wear yourself out." He paused. "What am I doing? Working. But thanks for asking."

She couldn't stop the smile that slipped out.

"Ha, there it is." Fisher raised his arms over his head. "We have a smile, people."

She shook her head, but she couldn't stop smiling. Which really irritated her. She needed to be more careful around him.

Two men came into the bar, and one nodded. "Fisher."

Kylee watched as the three exchanged the standard male-shoulder-slap thing that seemed to have replaced a customary handshake.

"Hey, pretty lady." One of them sat on the bar stool. "Jarvis is back."

She looked at him. "What does Jarvis want to drink?"

"A pint of stout." He grinned. "And an appetizer. But we can start with your number."

She pulled off a pint of beer, and placed the glass on the counter. "Your *drink*." She faced the other man and asked, "Going to try something other than a Dr. Pepper tonight?"

"Come on, Mario," Jarvis nudged him. "Man up."

Mario laughed. "No."

Kylee put a large glass with ice on the counter and nodded at the soda machine along the back wall. "You know where it is."

Mario nodded. "Thanks, Kylee."

The three took up their places at the pool table and Kylee got back to work.

People steadily streamed in. It was Thursday night, so most were locals. She was beginning to recognize a few faces. Thursdays were the night Janet and two other teachers came in for their "book club." But Kylee had listened to their conversations and she'd yet to hear them mention a single book.

There were plenty of customers from the university's vet school—like Fisher, Mario and Jarvis. Some were in scrubs, others not. She was beginning to tell the difference between the staffers and the upper-level students by their demeanor. The students all looked exhausted and stressed out.

Then there were ranch workers from Boone Ranch. Apparently the Boones were a pretty big deal in Stonewall Crossing, the founding family of the town and the veterinarian school. According to Cutter they owned most of the county and employed half the people who lived here. To own that much property, employ so many people, run a working ranch *and* run a bed-and-breakfast on part of their property, the Boones had to be loaded. The number of Boone employees she'd served supported that. Looking at Fisher it was hard to imagine the wealth he came from, he acted humble and…regular.

Her eyes swept the bar again. Normally a few patrons would sit at the bar and watch whatever sports Cutter put on. Tonight, one of them—a Boone employee—was worked up about something. He was radiating hostility, something she knew well. The rigid set of his jaw, the short, jerky movements—signs he might be trouble. She shook her head. What would be signs of trouble in Las Vegas didn't always apply here. Stonewall Crossing was a very different sort of town. Quiet and slow and peaceful. The sort of place she'd seen on television, dreamed of, but never expected to live in.

A chorus of laughter came from Cutter and his cronies. They played cards twice a week. They told bad jokes, laughed a little too loud—and were completely adorable. For all Cutter's outspoken opinions and cranky temperament, Kylee was getting pretty fond of her ancient landlord and savior.

Her eyes swept the room, taking in the expressions and actions of each customer. It was a habit she'd picked up when she was working with Jesse. Even though she wasn't looking for a handoff or someone who'd make an easy target, she still "cased the joint."

Only one thing stood out. The ranch worker in the corner was glaring at Fisher with pure, unfiltered aggression. The kind of aggression that usually didn't end well. Her gaze shifted to Fisher Boone, towering above every other man in the room. His cowboy hat was pushed back on his head and his eyes were narrowed as he watched Jarvis make the shot at the pool table. He had no clue he was being sized up for a takedown.

Whatever the problem was, Kylee hoped the ranch worker would reconsider. Fisher was a mountain of a man. He had a fit build, big hands and wasn't knocking back alcohol—the way this guy was. If there was a fight, Fisher would win.

"Big fellow," Cutter nudged her.

She nodded, proud that her boss's sudden appearance didn't have her jumping out of her skin.

"Good family, too. Lot of money and land." Cutter helped himself to a pint. "If a gal had any sense, she'd set her sights on landing that one."

She stared at Cutter then. "What?"

"You heard me." His leathered face creased with a grin.

"Guess I'm short on sense," she murmured.

"Not a troublemaker, either. Even if he is the size of a full-grown grizzly." He laughed.

"Well, trouble found him." Kylee nodded in the direction of the man shooting daggers at Fisher.

"George?" Cutter snorted. "Carson is always starting something with someone. Damn fool hothead. Let me know if his drinking gets out of hand. But I wouldn't worry your pretty lil head too much."

Good to know. Kylee studied the man. She had a list of rules for their new life in Stonewall Crossing. Number one, no men. Number two, avoid troublemakers. In her experience, however, the two were pretty much the same thing. She glanced at Carson again. Especially the troublemakers with tempers who drank too much.

Number three, become self-reliant. She was still working on number three. The first two were a lot easier to follow.

"Have any luck looking for a new job?"

She looked at Cutter again, frowning.

"Something with better hours. Be better for the boy, too. You can't enjoy working in this place all that much, while Shawn's hangin' out in the break room watchin' TV," he grumbled. "Or want to stay in that rattrap apartment."

Did Cutter want her to leave? Was he telling her it wasn't working? She knew having her preteen brother underfoot wasn't ideal, but what other choice did she have? He'd been good, spending more time drawing in his sketch pad than anything else. Shawn was what kept her going, kept her fighting. She didn't want to move him again. But if Cutter wanted them to move, to start over again, she'd figure it out.

A hollow emptiness formed in the pit of her stomach. If life had taught her one thing it was not to put down roots. Yet here she was, loving the tiny apartment she and Shawn shared. She didn't care that they lived behind a bar. Better than the nights they'd spent on the street. For the first time in her life, she and Shawn didn't have to worry about where they were going to sleep that night. They had an actual kitchen, not just a hot plate. And a bathroom they didn't have to share with everyone else on their floor.

But if Cutter wanted them out, it wasn't like she had a right to argue with him. She just needed to know. Her tone was cool as she asked, "Do you want us out of the apartment?"

"Did I say that?" Cutter scowled at her. "What the Sam Hill is that about?"

She twisted the towel in her hands. "I know you could get more rent than I can afford to pay you."

Cutter snorted loudly. "Don't give a rat's ass 'bout that. Never said you should leave. Or that you needed to find other work, either." He crossed his arms over his chest. "Givin' you options. Pointin' out a single fellow and a more respectable job doesn't mean I'm kicking you two out, ya hear?"

She relaxed, a little. "Oh." She glanced at Fisher, who happened to be looking at her, and frowned. "I… I appreciate you looking out for me." As far as she was concerned, her job was perfectly respectable. If Cutter knew what she'd done for Jesse… She shuddered.

Her hours at the bar weren't the best, but Shawn didn't mind staying in the break room watching TV and sketching after he'd finished the workbook pages she made him do. And Fisher? How could she explain that the last thing she wanted was a man to screw things up? Cutter might not get it, but as far as she was concerned, life was good. She smiled at the old man. "I can't thank you enough for what you've given me and Shawn—"

Cutter cut her off with a grunt. "You work hard, Kylee. I'm not giving you nothin'. Life shouldn't be so hard."

She gave Cutter an awkward one-armed hug. "Well… thanks. I'll get back to work."

"You're up." Jarvis leaned closer to whisper, "Try staring a little harder."

Fisher was a good foot taller than Jarvis so he made a point of looking down at him before quipping, "Watch out. I don't want to step on you." He wasn't staring at Kylee. He'd just been looking that way.

"Harsh, man," Jarvis sighed, stepping back. "You're the Sasquatch."

Fisher leaned across the table, lined up the cue ball and sent the green six ball into the upper-right corner pocket. Mario laughed, Jarvis groaned and Fisher searched out the next best shot. He adjusted his aim, leaned forward and set his cue.

But Jarvis's muttered, "Looks like Fisher isn't the only one interested in the new bartender," threw him off. He missed pocketing the yellow one. When he straightened, Jarvis was laughing.

Fisher scanned the bar, but all he saw was Cutter talking to Kylee. "You're cheating now?" he asked Jarvis.

Jarvis shrugged. "Didn't think it would work."

Fisher finished off his beer and glanced back toward Kylee. She was looking at him, frowning. He smiled at her, saluting her with his beer bottle. Not that she seemed to care. She turned away, her scowl still in place.

"Ouch," Mario whispered.

Fisher shrugged. "Can't win 'em all, I guess."

"You didn't even make it out of the starting gate with that one." Jarvis sounded way too pleased about that. "Must chap your hide, being rejected by something so curvy and soft. That long black hair. Those big blue eyes." Jarvis shook his head. "Maybe the lady's not into sasquatches. Maybe she likes normal-size guys." He elbowed Mario, who laughed—albeit reluctantly.

"You're just pissed I've been kicking your butt all night," Fisher said, laughing off their teasing. The three of them had been working together for years, but they'd been friends even longer. The kidding was part of it. So was his beating them at pool. But it wasn't about the winning, it was about the chance to relax after a long day.

Relaxation didn't exist once he got home—not since Archer had moved in. His brother needed a place to stay while the water pipes in his place were repaired. Since the family's Lodge was booked solid and his other two brothers had a families of their own, Fisher felt obliged to take him in. Problem was that Archer had only one setting: intense. If Fisher was spending more time at Shots, it was because he needed a break from his brother.

The new bartender didn't hurt, either. He was sure Kylee was the prettiest thing he'd ever seen. Even if she didn't like the looks of him.

They played a few hours, then moved on to darts. Fisher was one of the last to leave the bar. He lingered, slowly enjoying his beer. There were times he wished he had his younger brother Ryder's finesse with the ladies. Most of them thought Fisher was *cute* and flirted with him easily enough, but he'd never been all that interested in pursuing something more.

Jarvis's teasing had chapped his hide because few women caught his attention the way Kylee had. And she had. So much so that he found it hard not to openly stare at her as she swept the floor, mesmerized by her long black hair swaying as she worked. If she'd just look at him with the slightest flicker of interest he'd figure out some way to start up a conversation. Instead, she seemed oblivious to him. Once his beer was gone and the bar was empty, he had no reason to stay.

He put his empty bottle on the counter. "Night," he called out, making a last effort.

Kylee nodded but didn't look up, her black hair blocking her face from view. He walked out of the bar, glancing back at Kylee through the glass front of the door. She was still sweeping.

He stared up at the perfect circle of a moon hanging low in the deep black sky. A million stars broke up the canvas of dark. July in Texas was a scorcher, not that August and September were much better. And, from the feel of it, it was going to be a long, hot summer. But after the damn near arctic winter they'd had, he didn't mind so much. If anything, the chirp of the cicadas and crickets, and the thick, humid air was a pleasant change.

"Fisher Boone."

Fisher didn't recognize the slurred and angry voice until he turned around. "Carson." He nodded at George Carson, one of Archer's employees. He didn't know Carson but Archer didn't think too highly of him. "Everything all right?"

"Been better," Carson bit out, a hard smile on his face. "I need you to give your brother a message for me."

He nodded, realizing just how worked up George Carson was when the man's fist slammed into his right eye. Fisher was still recovering when the next hit came, catching him in the gut and knocking the air out of him. He shook his head, instinct taking over. He tried to rein himself in, to keep control. But with one punch, Carson was on the ground. Fisher groaned, "Dammit."

Suddenly Kylee stood there, staring down at Carson, a beer bottle in her hand.

Fisher wiped away the blood running into his eye, made sure Carson was breathing, then turned to Kylee. She held the neck of the bottle with a white-knuckle grip, her body shaking. "Got my back?" Fisher asked, still processing.

Kylee blinked, tossing the bottle into a garbage bin in the alley between the buildings. "Doesn't look like you needed it," she murmured. She looked at him and crossed her arms over her chest, rubbing her hands up and down her arms. "So, you're not a fighter, huh?"

His eye was throbbing. His fist…it hurt to flex his thumb, and from the way the muscles in his palm pulsed and burned, he suspected he'd dislocated it—again. "I didn't say I couldn't fight. I said I don't fight. My size gives me an unfair advantage." He'd learned that the hard way.

She nodded, her eyes searching his face. He wished he knew what was going on inside that head of hers. Even standing here bleeding, all he could do was grin at her. She stared at him, then shook her head. She stepped over the unconscious Carson and reached up to tilt his head back. "You're bleeding pretty bad." Her fingers settled on his temple, her eyes narrowing. "The light's better inside."

His hand encircled her wrist, brushing over her soft skin. She drew away immediately, stepping back and almost tripping over the man on the ground. Fisher caught her but released her instantly. Even with that slight contact, his hands tingled.

He cleared his throat. "He probably needs looking after more than I do." He nodded at George Carson, but he was too startled by how blue her gaze was to look away. Clear blue. Like a perfect summer sky. Or the surface of the lake.

She cocked an eyebrow at him. "You're going to patch him up?"

Better than standing around bleeding, thinking about how damn pretty she was. He nodded. "Have my bag in my truck."

"Why?" she asked.

"Why do I have my bag in my truck?" He wiped his eye, smiling at her. "I like to be prepared."

She put her hands on her hips, clearly not amused.

He glanced at Carson. "Can't just leave him here."

She stood there, confusion lining her face, while he collected his medical bag from his truck. He handed it to her and pulled George Carson inside the bar.

"Dumb ass," Cutter murmured as Fisher propped Carson in a chair. "You called it, Kylee. I'll call his brother to come get him. Got his number in the back." He wandered off, leaving Fisher to inspect Carson.

As far as Fisher could tell, Carson would wake up with a massive jaw ache and an impressive knot on the back of his thick skull. But that was about it. "He's going to feel that in the morning." Fisher glanced at Kylee. Her blue eyes were fixed on him, puzzling things out. She masked her expression when his gaze met hers, but he could sense the tension thrumming in her veins. "You okay?"

Her brow furrowed. She opened her mouth, then closed it. Her gaze bored into his, raw and intense.

He straightened, crossing to her. "Kylee?"

She stared up at him, her hands rubbing up and down her arms again. He reached for her, but she stepped back. He stopped, his hands falling to his sides. He'd no intention of scaring her, even though it was plain to see he did.

"Serves him right," Cutter barked, reappearing. Fisher watched Kylee march behind the bar, her movements jerky and tense. "His brother will be here in a shake or two," Cutter continued.

Fisher shook his head, placing his left hand on the counter. He stared at the bulging thumb, willing it to move. It didn't. It was an old injury. It didn't take much to pop it out—like it was now. There was no hope for it, he grabbed the metacarpal and, with one quick jerk, popped his thumb back into place. He winced.

"Damn boy," Cutter cursed loudly, slapping Fisher on his shoulder. "Could use some stitching, too, from the looks of it."

Kylee placed a bag of ice and a towel on the counter, a hint of sympathy in her eyes as she glanced his way.

Fisher nodded at her, wrapping the ice in the towel. "I have some glue that should take care of it. Be back." He took his bag and headed to the restroom, washing his hands and cleaning the cut. No avoiding a black eye tomorrow. He leaned forward, applied a small amount of glue along the split in the skin and pressed the cut edges together. He counted to ten before blinking. When he did, the glue held.

He packed up his bag and threw away his trash, replaying the evening. He had no idea why Carson had punched *him*—other than being drunk. And Kylee's reaction? What had set her off? Carson's attack? Or Fisher's one-hit knockout?

He paused, shaking his head. Maybe Jarvis was right. He had to be more than a little interested in Kylee if he was worrying about her while he was supergluing his eyelid back together. He shook his head, double-checked the cut was sealed and washed up before heading back into the bar.

Kylee was opening the Staff Only door at the end of the hallway. She glanced at him, but didn't stop to say good-night.

"Thanks for the help," he said.

The door closed without her making a peep.

He shook his head, too tired and sore to worry about anything other than getting home and into bed.

Chapter Two

"I know your brother Ryder's given up his wild ways, but that doesn't mean you need to take his place," Teddy Boone said, grinning at Fisher.

Fisher reined in his horse, Waylon, tipped his cowboy hat back and shot his father a look. "Yep, set out lookin' for trouble last night—"

"Well, it looks like you found some." Teddy chuckled. "At least your face did." He shook his head. "Bet it hurts like hell."

Fisher nodded. "I'll survive. Even if I am up two hours before my shift to track down strays with you."

"A swollen eye won't get in the way of riding," his father argued.

"Seeing, maybe," Fisher answered, not minding the early-morning excursion in the least but knowing his dad expected some sass from him.

"Both my eyes are working just fine. You just follow my lead, son." Fisher saw his father give him one final assessing gaze before nudging his horse into a trot. "Herd was in the south pasture so I figure that's where they are."

"Expecting some calves?" Fisher asked. It was common enough for the heifers close to delivering to wander off until the calf was steady on his feet.

"Expect so," his father answered. "What, exactly, happened last night?"

Fisher drew Waylon alongside his father's horse, Chip, wincing when his thumb brushed the saddle horn. "George Carson."

"George Carson?" His father raised an eyebrow. "His daddy John Carson?"

Fisher shrugged.

"John Carson was a mean drunk."

"Then chances are the two of them are related," Fisher answered.

"What did you do?" his father asked.

"Knocked him out," Fisher answered, his jaw rigid.

Teddy chuckled. "I imagine you did. But I was asking why he felt the need to use your face for a punching bag."

Fisher didn't know what had transpired between Archer and George Carson. But he did know Archer and their father had a strained relationship. Teddy Boone thought Archer was an odd duck—worrying more over the care of his horse refuge than the people in his life. While Fisher agreed Archer marched to the beat of his own drum, he suspected Archer would do anything for his family. No point in adding fuel to the conflict between father and son when the ruckus with George Carson was over and done with.

"Not sure," Fisher said, which was mostly true.

"That right there is why I don't drink," Teddy said. "A man shouldn't put himself in a position to lose control. Damn fool thing to do." His father clicked his tongue and Chip's pace picked up, turning into a full-blown gallop.

Fisher didn't argue. But he knew firsthand a man could lose control without drinking. He lived with that knowledge every damn day. Dwelling on unpleasant memories didn't make much sense, so he concentrated on keeping up with his father for the next hour. There was no denying his father's disappointment when their search was unsuccessful.

"They'll turn up when they're ready, I guess," Teddy said before they parted ways.

"I'll check again tonight," Fisher volunteered. "If they haven't turned up by then."

Fisher turned Waylon out to pasture, took a quick shower and pulled himself together, cleaning the cut on his eye before heading into the vet hospital. Once he'd deposited his things in his office, he slipped on his lab coat and headed into the lounge for coffee.

"What happened to your face?" Archer glanced over the rim of his reading glasses.

"George Carson," Fisher mumbled, pouring a cup of coffee. He nodded at one of the vet techs walking through the hospital lounge, grinning at her startled expression. His eye looked worse than it felt—but it hurt pretty damn bad.

"Carson?" Archer frowned. "I fired him yesterday."

Fisher sat his cup down, taking care not to jostle his thumb. "That makes sense." He'd have to get Mario to splint it, to support the ligament. "He wanted me to deliver a message to you."

Archer's eyebrows rose.

Fisher pointed to his face. "Message."

Archer nodded, turning his attention back to the medical journal he was reading. "He's a jerk."

Fisher chuckled, wincing from the bruise on his stomach. Archer wasn't emotional, he knew that. But a "sorry" or "that sucks" or something that resembled sympathy would have been nice. Calling Carson a jerk was an understatement. He waited for more but Archer was silently reading again so he asked, "What did he do?"

"Drinking on the job," Archer answered. "He doesn't want the job, I'll find someone who will. Can't risk anyone's safety, animals or employees."

Fisher couldn't argue with his brother. There was no excuse for that sort of thing. He glanced at the clock. Almost time for morning rounds. "Anything exciting today?" he asked his brother. Archer only worked in the hospital a couple of days a week, spending most of his time at the animal refuge and rehabilitation center he operated on his part of Boone Ranch.

Archer shrugged. "Not that I know of."

"I'll let you know if something rolls in," Fisher offered. "Have a good one."

Archer nodded, flipping the page on his journal.

He headed straight for the operating room, hoping to catch Mario or Jarvis before any procedures got underway.

"I knew she wasn't interested, but I never thought she'd beat you up," Jarvis teased, staring at his face.

"Got time to tape this?" Fisher held up his hand and shook his head. "Or are you too busy thinking of smart-ass comebacks?"

Jarvis took in the violently colored bruising along Fisher's thumb. "What did you do, man?"

"She takes thumb wars really seriously," Fisher quipped, pointing at his eye. "She didn't like losing."

Jarvis laughed, setting to work on Fisher's thumb. "X-ray it?" he asked. "Might need a ligament repair."

Fisher shook his head. "It'll be fine."

"Dr. Fisher." One of his students stuck her head in. "We need you up front."

Fisher nodded. "What is it?"

"Stray." Abigail paused. "Are you okay?" She glanced at him. "You—"

"The patient?"

"Right. Sorry." But she couldn't stop staring at his face. "Dog with several deep bites along the neck and back leg. Ear laceration, almost bitten off. His right eye looks pretty bad, too."

"Bites from?" he asked.

"Two other dogs, apparently. Miss…" she paused to scan her notes. "Miss James just brought him in."

He nodded, following Abigail from the operating room and into the patient care room. A speckled dog lay on a metal table, his gray coat matted with blood and dirt. At first glance, he looked like a blue heeler, same size and build. The dog didn't raise his head when Fisher approached the table, though his uninjured eye was open and alert.

"Can you tell me what happened?" Fisher turned to the woman standing nervously in the corner. "Kylee?"

Was it his imagination or did she seem to relax when she saw him?

"Hi, Doc… Fisher." Her arms were crossed tightly over her bloodstained, oversize white T-shirt. "I was walking around the park and these two big dogs were on him. He was fighting so hard. But they were too big for him. I saw him go down beneath them…"

Fisher listened to the dog's heart rate with his stethoscope. Accelerated. One hundred ten. Respirations were shallow and rapid, distressed. But, from the number of injuries the animal had sustained, that was to be expected.

"No owners?" Abigail asked, taking notes on her clipboard.

"There wasn't anyone else in the park." Kylee glanced at Abigail, watching as she jotted down a few more notes. "No collar."

He continued his inspection of the dog, his hands gentle, yet probing. "How did you break them up?"

"I found a big stick." Her clear blue gaze held his, making it impossible not to look at her.

"A stick?" he repeated, trying to keep his voice neutral.

Her nod was tight. She was nervous, defiant...and so damn beautiful. He noticed her tension. It wasn't the first time he'd seen her this way. Why did she always seem ready to run? "It was a very big stick."

Abigail stopped writing then, looking at Kylee with the same mix of awe and surprise that he felt.

He shook his head. "You could have been seriously injured."

Kylee's face shuttered instantly. "All I had to do was yell and wave it at them, and they ran. He didn't."

Fisher wanted to tell her she was lucky. To tell her not to do it again. To shake her a little for putting herself at risk like that. But something told him that would be a mistake. Instead he said, "Abigail, make sure X-ray is free, please."

Once Abigail left, he spoke. "Dogs, especially when they're worked up like this, don't always respond predictably. You could be the one in the hospital, Kylee." His eyes swept over her too-big clothes and worn tennis shoes. Her black hair was pulled up in a ponytail that swung between her shoulders when she moved. She looked young and lost.

If she was listening to him, she gave no sign. Instead,

she stepped closer to the exam table, running her hand down the dog's side. "Will he be okay?"

"Not sure." He watched her, moved by the tenderness on her face. She was tough. And fearless. And, apparently, she had no problem defending the underdog. A flash of her holding that beer bottle sprang to mind. She'd been ready to defend him, too. Was that how she saw him? Someone who needed protecting? He couldn't stop his smile. "I'm sure he'd thank you if he could."

She glanced at him, a hint of a smile on her mouth. "I thought you were fluent in dog."

He laughed, surprised.

The dog whimpered and Kylee looked at him. "I feel like I should do something."

"Talk to him," Fisher encouraged. "It helps."

Kylee glanced at him, then bent forward to whisper something to the animal.

"X-ray is ready for him," Abigail said, poking her head into the exam room.

Fisher nodded, watching Kylee. "I'll take care of him," he promised her.

Kylee stepped back, crossing her arms over her chest again. "I can't… I don't have any money. He's a stray."

"It's a teaching hospital." Fisher nodded. "We'll take care of him. Cases like this are good learning opportunities."

She brightened. "Oh. Good." She glanced down at the dog. "He deserves a second chance."

He didn't miss the wistfulness in her voice or the flash of pain in her huge blue eyes. But, like the night before, she seemed to stop and pull into herself.

Jarvis came in, followed by two vet students. He saw Kylee and smiled. "Beating up the doctor one day and saving the dog in distress the next," he teased Kylee. "I imagine you make a mighty fine avenging angel."

She stared at Fisher, stunned. "I didn't touch Dr. Boone," she argued, glaring at him with such anger he wanted to throttle Jarvis. "But the dog…well, it wasn't a fair fight."

He'd have to worry over Kylee later. Right now he had a patient to tend to. And a group of vet students waiting for his direction. The students carefully lifted the dog, laying him gently on the gurney. Fisher turned the dog's head, assessing the injured eye. It didn't look good. But the lacerations that covered the dog's haunches and chest looked relatively superficial. He knew the students were watching, echoing his every motion, hanging on his every expression. It was part of the process, reading the animals, their owners, filling in the blanks when possible.

He stepped back. "Where do we start?" Fisher asked the three students, already clicking into teaching mode.

"Check his vitals," Abigail sounded off.

"Done," Fisher countered.

Jake, another student, was scanning the dog's chart. "Oxygen?"

Fisher waited, prompting them, "And?"

"Fluids," Abigail jumped in.

"IV?" Cliff asked.

Fisher nodded. "Good. And get him prepped for X-rays. Let's get to it." He held the door open, letting them lead the way.

Jarvis piped up, "We'll take him from here, Kylee. Don't worry, I have a feeling Dr. Fisher will do everything he can to see this mutt pulls through."

Fisher shot Jarvis a look, but his friend just winked on his way out. Kylee followed, pointedly avoiding eye contact as she brushed past him into the hallway. Her heat, her scent, washed over him—knocking him completely off center. He stood, rooted to the spot, staring after her swinging ponytail. But her blue eyes were fixed on the dog as it disappeared into the X-ray room. He saw the slight tremor in her shoulders, the way her hands fisted at her sides, and knew this dog was somehow important to her. He had one option—save the dog. For Kylee.

"WHAT DID HE SAY?" Cutter asked, spinning his worn hat in his hands.

"Is he gonna be okay, Kylee?" Shawn's voice shook.

She shrugged. "Dr. Boone said he'll do what he can."

"Which one?" Cutter asked. "There are two Dr. Boones in Stonewall Crossing."

"Fisher," she clarified. "Not much we can do now."

"Good. That's good," Cutter murmured, heading toward the admissions desk.

She tried to act unaffected, like it was every day she charged at two massive dogs screaming her head off. She didn't even know why she did it, exactly. That dog's desperation, trying again and again to get away, tore at something deep inside of her. She knew how that dog felt.

One glance at Shawn's terrified face had forced her into action. For the first time, she could actually chase away his fear…and save the dog. Once the bigger dogs were on the run, the little pup stood on unsteady legs, looked at her, wagged his tail, and fell over. She'd picked him up and hurried back to Cutter's place with Shawn running at her side.

Shawn's pleading had prompted Cutter to pack them into his beaten-up four-door Bronco and drive them to the veterinary hospital. He hadn't said much, all grunts and head shakes. But it didn't matter, they got there.

It was only after she'd laid the poor dog on the table that she realized what she'd done. Those dogs could have turned on her. Or Shawn. Her actions had put Shawn in real danger—over a dog. Danger Fisher had reminded her of.

She pulled her brother into a quick hug. Neither was all that comfortable with physical affection, but she needed comfort. If anything happened to her, where would that leave Shawn? She couldn't think about what might have happened. They were all they had. "Sorry I freaked out like that."

Shawn smiled up at her. "It was awesome." He laughed. "I was sorta scared of you for a minute."

She sighed. "I guess that was the point. Not to scare you, but the dogs."

"Come check these out." Shawn waved her toward the massive aquarium in the wall. "There's a puffer fish in here. And an eel, too."

Kylee stared, amazed by the vibrant colors of the agile creatures. She smiled as Shawn held a finger close to the glass and the fishes swam toward it. He moved his finger slowly and the little group of fishes followed. He glanced back at her, smiling. "Bet they think I'm going to feed 'em."

The doors of the vet school slid open and a young couple came in. The man cradled something, wrapped in a large beach towel, against his chest.

"We found this, when we were out walking." The young man placed the towel on the admissions counter.

"Do you remember where you found it?" the admissions clerk asked. "You need to remember exactly where you found it and put it back."

Shawn moved forward, but Kylee caught him by the shoulder. She led him around the side, so they could see but not get in the way. In the towel was a small deer, covered in white spots.

"We were in the park…" The young woman looked at the young man. "But I don't remember where, exactly."

The woman at the admissions desk frowned. "Momma probably dropped it there. But they come back, once they've found food. Fawns know how to hide and stay still, it's in their DNA."

"What happens if we don't put it in the right spot?" the young man asked.

The admissions clerk shook her head. "It'll starve."

"Oh." The young woman was really upset. "I told you we should have left it—"

"There were fire ants," the young man argued.

"Hold on." The woman at the counter buzzed, "Dr. Archer to the front, please."

"What'll happen?" Shawn whispered.

"Dr. Archer Boone works with all sorts of animals," the admissions clerk explained, smiling at Shawn. "He has a big ol' refuge on the Boone Ranch. It's mostly abandoned or abused horses, but he also takes in local wildlife that need tending. He had a skunk. Oh, and a squirrel. And normally a few fawns on a bottle, too."

Dr. Archer walked through the swinging doors. He barely acknowledged the people in the room, heading straight for the fawn. *This* was Fisher's brother?

Kylee couldn't help but notice how different Archer was from Fisher. Both were tall, but Fisher was *bigger*. Fisher was thick and broad—built like a fighter. He was a fighter, that much was clear. Knocking Carson out with one punch without losing his cool…it had been impressive and unnerving all at the same time. She didn't see Archer doing something like that. Sure, he was fit, but more like a runner. And his face…his face wasn't as expressive—as warm—as his brother's. Not that she'd met many men like Fisher Boone.

"Found it?" Dr. Archer asked, seeing their answering nods. "Fire ants?" He lifted the fawn. It made an impressively loud sound, and Shawn covered his ears.

Kylee watched the way Archer assessed the animal. "Donna," he spoke to the admissions clerk, "have them sign the drop-off form. I'll go ahead and take it back."

Donna pulled out a clipboard and pen, offering it to the couple.

"What will happen to it?" Shawn asked.

Archer glanced at Shawn. "We'll shelter him until he's ready for release."

Shawn nodded, his attention bouncing between Dr. Boone and the fawn. She knew what the look on her brother's face meant. A thousand questions were coming. He started with, "What do you mean? Shelter?"

"Shawn, he's got work to do," Kylee said, trying to reel in her little brother and his endless fascination.

"Oh." Shawn nodded. "Right."

Dr. Archer almost smiled before he carried the deer into the back. Kylee watched. If it had been Fisher, she suspected he'd have answered all of Shawn's questions. Chances were he'd have taken Shawn into the back and shown him around. She paused, wondering where the hell that had come from. She had no idea what Fisher would do. And more importantly, she didn't care.

"Kylee," Cutter waved her toward the admissions desk. "This is Donna. She's looking to retire in…?"

"Right before Christmas. Five months, two weeks and about seventy hours," Donna said, shaking Kylee's hand. "Cutter said you might be interested in applying for the position?"

"That'd be cool." Shawn nodded, his blue eyes inspecting the waiting room and check-in desk. "Learn about helping animals and stuff."

"It is pretty cool." Donna winked at Shawn before turning back to Kylee. "Money's not bad. Hours are regular, rarely any overtime—that falls to the student workers who come on in the evenings for emergency duty. You get school holidays, which is nice when you have family." She winked at Shawn. "It can get a little hairy now and then, but I guess working at the bar you've seen it all. Oh, and you get health care and retirement, too. And tuition reimbursement, if you want to go back to school."

Kylee was speechless. She had no intention of applying for this job. But hearing the laundry list of reasons why she should apply gave her pause. A real job? Health benefits, normal hours, and vacation time with Shawn. She glanced at her brother, who was looking at her. She knew that look, that how-can-you-say-no? look. How *could* she say no?

She shook her head. She didn't have a vehicle, for one, and it would be a long walk from the bar to the vet hospital. "I'm not so sure," she spoke up. "I don't have much experience with computers. Or animals."

"I'd train you. It's not hard—most of the programs are tailored for the school. You just gotta stay on top of things." Donna shrugged. "And be nice to customers. They're real uppity about being *nice to the customers*."

Which was another problem. Kylee was civil but nice was a stretch.

Shawn snorted. "Never mind."

Donna and Cutter laughed, too.

"Hey." But she was smiling, too. "I thought you were on my side."

"I am." Shawn stared around the lobby. He was clearly impressed. But then, he hadn't spent much of his life in a place this interesting—or clean. "You should work here."

Her gaze followed his, taking in the detailed mural that ran around the top of the waiting room. It was gorgeous, a rainbow of subtly faded colored animals. Between the fish tank and the sliding glass doors into the clinic, there was a light and airy openness. Maybe that was why she felt nervous? The bar was dim and small, easier to hide in. She knew to be on guard and what to look for. But here? Working here would put her on display, front and center. Easy to find, if someone was looking.

"Just in case." Donna slid several sheets of paper across the counter. "Here's the application."

Shawn nudged her until she picked up the papers. "Thanks."

"Better be gettin' back," Cutter interrupted. "Got a bar to run."

THE WEEK FLEW BY. Fisher was in charge of the spay clinic on Tuesdays and neuter clinic on Thursdays. Wednesday and Friday classes were followed by afternoon clinical rotations. Every day he checked on Kylee's sweet-natured stray. The clinic had named him Chance—because he'd been given a second chance. He hadn't lost the eye, but he had lost most of his ear. His back leg wasn't broken, but the tissue and skin had been badly damaged. Chance had more stitches than Fisher cared to count. The dog would heal, but his gait would probably always be a little off. All things considering, Fisher was pleased things had turned out so well.

By the time quitting time rolled around Friday, he was glad he didn't have emergency duty that weekend. His thumb was better, but still tender. And next week he'd need full range of motion to handle Goliath for his post-op visit. He and the giant rottweiler didn't see eye to eye when it came to who was alpha in the room. It didn't help that Goliath's hundred-pound owner spoiled the beast. But it was time to check the damn dog's pins and he was the only doctor who would still work with him, so resting his thumb was necessary.

Besides, a few days off from the hospital was a good thing. Not that his father would let him sit around and do nothing. Nope, Teddy Boone had a never-ending list of things to be done on the ranch. Cutting cedar, replacing fence stays, grading the back road that had washed out during the winter rains and rounding up calves were on the old man's agenda. But tonight Fisher was going to enjoy himself.

Every weekend Cutter opened the dance hall off the bar, bringing a good portion of Stonewall Crossing out to enjoy the live music and family-friendly atmosphere. His brother Ryder had invited the whole family to the Shots dance hall that night.

His brothers—minus Archer—their wives and his cousins from Montana would all be there. Ryder's wife, Annabeth, was getting close to delivering their twins so there weren't a lot of nights out in their future. Annabeth wasn't really up to dancing, but he suspected Ryder and their young son, Cody, were trying to cheer her up. She'd been pretty uncomfortable the last few weeks.

Knowing he'd see Kylee was an added incentive. She was a prickly little thing, someone he didn't understand— yet. But that hadn't stopped him from thinking about her throughout the week or hoping he'd see her when she checked in on Chance.

"Eye's lookin' better," Cutter greeted him as he walked into the bar.

"Thanks. Feelin' a bit better, too." Fisher smiled.

"Here's hoping this weekend is downright unevent- ful," Cutter laughed.

"No arguments from me," Fisher agreed, heading through the open doors and into the dance hall in back.

Most of his family was there already, crowded together around two tables. They smiled, waving him over.

"What happened to you?" Renata, his twin sister, was on her feet. "And why didn't I know about it?" She frowned at her brothers.

"Nothing to tell, really." Fisher hugged her.

"Way I hear it, he took one in the eye for Archer." Ryder, the youngest Boone, grinned.

"First his roommate, now his stunt double," his cousin Tandy said, wincing and shaking her head. "Archer owes you big time, cuz."

"I'm with Tandy. Being the oldest means I have to look out for all of you, but—" his big brother, Hunter, pointed at Fisher's eye "—taking a punch to the face for Archer is going above and beyond brotherly duty." Hunter grinned. "I'm betting Archer didn't shoulder much guilt over it. Or is he coming to buy you a thank-you beer later?"

"Nope," Ryder shook his head. "He bowed out, something about some new something-or-other at the refuge needing his attention."

"He needs a girlfriend," Renata sighed.

Fisher, Ryder and Hunter burst out laughing.

"Hey, Fish— Your face!" Annabeth, Ryder's very pregnant wife arrived, almost dropping the pitcher of water she carried.

"He's fine, princess." Ryder stood and pulled a chair back for her. "Don't get yourself all worked up."

Annabeth rolled her eyes.

"What are we laughing over?" Josie, Hunter's wife, joined in. "I'm assuming it's not Fisher's face?"

"Sort of." Hunter kissed his wife's cheek.

"I was just saying Archer might benefit from the company of a lady friend," Renata offered.

"What about the new bartender?" Annabeth asked. "She's gorgeous."

"She is, at that." Toben, his cousin and Tandy's twin, tipped his beer bottle at the bar. "I don't think Archer could handle that one."

"Kylee and Archer? As a couple?" Fisher asked before he could stop himself. He didn't like the way Toben was looking at her. He heard the shock in his voice, and so did everyone else around the table. He didn't miss the grins the women exchanged.

"Kylee, huh?" Hunter piped up, hiding his smile behind his beer.

Ryder was looking at him wide-eyed. "Huh," he murmured before craning his neck to see the bar at the back of the room. "Where is she?"

"Working at the back bar," Annabeth answered. "Long black hair. Biggest blue eyes. Other than yours, of course." She grabbed Ryder's chin and pressed a kiss to his lips.

Fisher watched, seeing the satisfied smile on his little brother's face. His brother, the player…he never thought he'd see his brother so happily settled, but then Fisher had never had a woman look at him the way Annabeth was looking at Ryder. "Guess I'll get a beer," he mumbled, pushing himself up from his chair.

Which led to a few giggles from the women.

He didn't respond as he made his way across the dance hall, smiling and exchanging pleasantries as he went.

Kylee didn't see him, she was busy filling mugs and popping tops off beer bottles. Cutter didn't serve hard liquor when the dance hall was open—only beer, water and soda. Cutter said it kept things from getting out of control and was more family friendly.

"What can I—?" She paused, her gaze meeting his. She caught sight of his face and wrinkled her nose.

"Evening, Kylee," he said, smiling.

"Doc." She nodded. "How's the dog?"

"Getting stronger. Jarvis said you've stopped by a couple of times. Sorry I missed you." He smiled. "You should come see him again. Nothing perks a fella's spirits up like a visit from a pretty lady."

Her eyes narrowed.

He held his hands up. "*He* told me to say that."

"He? As in, the dog?" Kylee asked, smiling even though he could tell she tried like hell not to.

"Yep." He nodded. "The dog."

"Good to know he's feeling well enough to talk." She shook her head, looking uncomfortable as she murmured, "Thank you for looking after him." She was pretty when she blushed. Who was he kidding? She was pretty all the time. Especially when she wasn't frowning at him.

"Hey, lady, can we get a beer?" someone called from the other end of the bar.

"Cutter got you workin' alone?" he asked.

"Joni called in sick." Kylee shrugged. "Meaning her boyfriend is in town. Bobby's coming in about an hour." And with that, she went back to work.

"How'd I know I'd find you here?" Jarvis asked, sitting on one of the bar stools. "You should know, your whole family is watching."

"More reason to stay here." He sighed.

"Fisher," Kylee called out, sliding his preferred beer down the bar toward him.

He grabbed the bottle—even though he hadn't told her what he wanted. He shouldn't read too much into it. She was a good bartender and he'd been a regular customer. That's all. A bartender who was working…so he should leave her alone and stop giving his family a reason to talk.

"Feel free to join me." He pointed to his family. "My cousins are new in town. I can introduce you to Tandy, if you promise to behave."

"Making no promises," Jarvis said.

Fisher took his beer, trying to dodge a group of kids—his nephew Eli, Hunter's son, included—and stepped back, bumping into something. He turned to find a boy bent over, collecting papers and shoving them into a notebook.

"Sorry, mister," the boy murmured, looking up at him.

"No problem." He stooped beside the boy, picking up several papers. The boy liked horses; he'd drawn a lot of them. One in particular caught Fisher's eye.

"I'll meet you over there," Jarvis said, leaving him for his very blonde, very pretty cousin.

Fisher nodded, still inspecting the sketch. "Did you draw these?"

The kid nodded, thick black hair flopping onto his forehead.

"These are really great." Something about the kid was familiar. "Having fun?"

The boy's smile was small, almost nervous, as his clear blue gaze met Fisher's. "Yeah, I guess."

He helped the boy pick everything up before offering the boy his hand. "Fisher Boone."

The boy's eyes went round. "You're Doc Fisher?" The boy looked him up and down.

"Hey, Uncle Fisher," Eli showed up. "Hey, Shawn."

"Hey, yourself." Fisher grinned at his nephew, then glanced back at the boy. "And who are you?"

"He's Shawn, Kylee's brother," Eli offered up.

Shawn nodded in the direction of the bar. "The crazy dog-lady bartender. That's my sister."

Kylee had a little brother? It was obvious now. They both had black hair and blue eyes—and they both seemed nervous, wound too tight. What they were nervous about, he had no idea. Knowing she had a younger brother here with her was a surprise. Were they on their own? Shawn couldn't be that much older than Eli. He had the gangly height and loose limbs of a boy on the cusp of manhood. Where were their parents?

"Nice to meet you," Fisher said, glancing at Kylee. She worked with quick efficiency, at ease behind the bar. She was a puzzle, a beautiful puzzle. Meeting Shawn to-night reminded him there was a lot he didn't know about her—a lot he wanted to know. "You've got a pretty cool sister," he added.

Shawn nodded.

"Your face looks like it hurts, Uncle Fisher," Eli said, shaking his head.

"You should see the other guy," Fisher teased.

"Kylee said you knocked him out with one punch." Shawn seemed impressed.

Fisher's gaze returned to Kylee. So she'd told her brother. And while he didn't want Shawn to think fighting was a good thing, he couldn't deny it pleased him to know she had mentioned him to Shawn. She looked up then, her gaze searching the dance hall until she found Shawn. Fisher could see her relief from where he stood. Once more he pondered what would make her so anxious, almost like she was running from something. Or someone.

Her blue gaze met his. He lifted an eyebrow, pointing at Shawn with a grin. She smiled and it almost brought him to his knees. It was a real smile, given freely and withholding nothing. She loved her little brother with everything she had. And damn if he wouldn't give everything to have her smiling over him like that.

"Fisher?" Eli waved a hand in front his face. "Fisher?"

He forced his attention from the beauty behind the bar. "What's up?"

"What was the fight over?" Eli asked.

Fisher shook his head. "George Carson was upset and I was the one he decided to take it out on."

"His mistake." Shawn was looking at him with the same intensity Kylee had. "Sounds like a hothead."

Fisher nodded, wondering how many hotheads were in Kylee and Shawn's past.

"Come on." Eli pushed Shawn's shoulder. "You can draw later."

Shawn shoved his sketchbook into the worn canvas bag slung over his shoulder. "Okay."

"Y'all have fun." Fisher smiled. "But stay out of trouble."

"Yes, sir," Eli said. Shawn nodded, giving his sister a quick wave. Fisher glanced back at Kylee, catching sight of her sweet smile again. When she smiled like that, he couldn't do a thing but stare at her.

Renata joined him. "Looks like Archer's out of luck," she murmured.

Fisher frowned at his sister. "Aw, come on, Renata—"

"You might as well stop now. I know you, baby brother. You're done for." She was born three minutes before he was and loved to use her "seniority" when able. She patted his arm. "And if you keep looking at her like that, everyone's going to know it. You've never had much of a poker face."

Chapter Three

Fisher dropped to his knees in the parking lot of the vet school, keeping well away from the edge of the beat-up Jeep. A growl greeted him. His gaze met that of the very angry, very disoriented bobcat crouched smack-dab in the middle under the Jeep. Dammit.

"He's in the middle," Fisher announced, seeing two pairs of vet students' feet—too far back to do much good. He knew these kids were scared, and he didn't blame them. But if this was going to be their job they needed to learn how to handle difficult situations with hostile animals. Technically, it was a pretty sweet training opportunity. This was one of the reasons he loved his job—he liked a little danger now and then. As long as everything turned out right in the end. Just now, they needed to help this animal. The bobcat was breathing hard, clearly in distress.

"I need the catch pole," Fisher called out, but the students' feet didn't move.

The cat looked around nervously.

"Now," he spoke again, trying to keep things calm. If they didn't get the animal lassoed, it would end up running onto the highway. He didn't want to see that happen.

The vet students' feet moved, both of them.

"One of you needs to stay there," he spoke again while mentally cursing the situation. Where was Archer? He could use some experienced backup on this one—just in case.

The cat's ears perked up as it looked at him.

Fisher smiled. "Don't suppose you'd let me take you inside? So we can get you fixed up?"

The cat lay down, still panting.

"Here, Dr. Boone." The vet student handed down the catch pole.

"Nope, get on your knees and see what we're doing." Fisher didn't take his eyes off the cat. Bobcats were fast.

"But—"

"What's your name?" Fisher asked.

"Michelle," she said.

"Well, Michelle, I can see it. And it needs help." He paused. "That's your job, right?"

A few seconds later Michelle was on her knees beside him. "It's gorgeous."

"It is. But remember it's also a pissed off wild animal with a nasty set of claws and teeth. I wouldn't get all warm and fuzzy over it." Fisher knew all too well the havoc a bobcat could wreak on a farm. A few years back, he'd spent the better part of an afternoon cleaning up what remained of the family chicken coop after a bobcat's visit. It hadn't been pretty. "You need to get the pole in front of it. Keep it flat, slide it in—"

He kept his voice low and even, for the cat and Michelle. When it came time to catch the cat, he took the pole. He was quick, flipping the loop over the cat's head and snugging the loop before the animal could react. When it realized it was caught, the bobcat dug in, the growl deafening.

"Tranquilizer?" Fisher asked.

"Jake has it." Fisher could hear the awe and fear in Michelle's voice as the bobcat thrashed around.

Fisher sighed. "Maybe now would be a good time for him to use it?" This was ridiculous. "Before it makes its injuries worse?"

"Jake," Michelle called out. "Now. Sedate him."

Jake flopped down on his stomach on the other side of the vehicle. Fisher pulled the noose just tight enough to keep the animal still so Jake could get a solid shot from the tranq gun, praying the kid knew how to aim. A minute later the bobcat was unconscious, completely limp.

"I'll get a gurney," Michelle offered, hurrying in to the hospital.

"Sorry, man," Jake murmured, joining Fisher. "Guess I sort of panicked."

"In a situation like this, you've got to focus and stay calm." Fisher needed Jake to understand how serious things were. "You've got a highway, pedestrians, a tranq gun—a lot of variables in an uncontrolled environment. You have to act quickly—carefully."

Jake's shoulder drooped.

"Good shot, though," Fisher added.

Jake nodded.

The two of them pulled the forty-plus-pound animal from under the Jeep and onto the sidewalk, out of harm's way. Fisher rubbed the cat's head, checking its pupils before running his hands along its muscular side. The cat's right back leg hung at an awkward angle.

"Fracture. Possibly oblique, maybe transverse. We'll know soon," he murmured.

"Pretty lucky, considering." Jake knelt beside him.

Fisher nodded. "So was the woman who was driving."

Why the woman decided to put the bobcat into the Jeep with her after she'd hit it, he'd never know. Sure, she did a good thing by bringing it to the hospital. But she'd also endangered herself by handling a wild animal. She'd loaded it into her Jeep while it was too stunned to react. But when it did come round, the bobcat wasn't too thrilled about being trapped. The woman was going to need stitches the length of her forearm as well as on her thigh and the side of her hand. The bobcat was probably looking at some pins and a plate in his leg.

Michelle arrived, pushing the metal gurney in front of her. "Sorry. Couldn't find one big enough."

Fisher stood, scooping the bobcat up and placing it on the gurney. "No problem. Long as we get him into a cage before he wakes up again." He ran his hands over the bobcat, careful of the broken leg. "Did you page Dr. Archer?"

Michelle paused. "No."

"I will." Jake finished making notes on his tablet and started to go, but Fisher stopped him.

"How about you two get the cat secured first." He shot a meaningful look at Jake. Something about fourth-year vet students. They got all competitive. "Then call Dr. Archer to present the case—together."

Jake looked irritated, but he nodded and helped Michelle push the gurney inside.

He followed behind the two, making a few notes on his tablet. When he entered the hospital he was hit with a chorus of barking. It was vaccination day. The community clinic in the teaching hospital offered a low-cost vaccination clinic once a month. Cats in the morning and dogs in the afternoon. He glanced at his watch. It was almost four. From the looks of the lobby, they were behind.

"Hey, Dr. Fisher," Shawn's voice caught him off guard. "Kylee said Chance wanted to see us so we brought him a toy." The boy held up a large rawhide twist.

He smiled at Shawn. "Good to see you, Shawn. Chance's gonna be one happy dog." His eyes swept the room until he found Kylee. She stood off to the side, arms crossed, posture rigid. Like him, she was inspecting the room—but she wasn't looking for him. He didn't know what she was looking for, but it was obvious she wasn't comfortable being there. He and Shawn joined her. "Hi."

"Hi," she murmured, hardly acknowledging him.

"What?" he teased, cupping his ear.

She looked at him, her eyes so blue they took his breath away. "I said hi."

"What?" he repeated, loudly. "Wait." He waved them through the doors that separated the lobby from the exam rooms and specialty wings. "Hi."

She arched a brow. "You think you're funny, don't you?"

"I have my moments. You have to admit, it's a little quieter back here." He smiled. "Let me take you back to see Chance."

She nodded, a small smile on her face. In the few days since he'd seen her, he'd thought a lot about her smile. "Is it always this crowded?"

He shook his head. "Last Monday of the month we have discounted vaccinations. Tends to be our busiest day of the month."

"Oh." Her expression softened further. "That's really nice."

"We try to do that around here," he returned. "Be nice. Take care of animals. And their people."

"What was that thing on the cart?" Shawn asked, pointing at the gurney and its comatose occupant.

"It's a bobcat," Kylee answered. Her huge blue gaze fixed on him, "Right?"

"Yep." Fisher nodded, inspecting her. She looked tired, with dark circles under her eyes. But then, working all night would do that to a person. How she managed her job and kept up with Shawn was a mystery. Looking at her, he'd bet she could use a break. It was close enough to quitting time—maybe he could take them for an ice cream.

She'd say no, he knew that. She was too guarded. But he'd already learned she had two soft spots. Her brother and animals. He respected her desire to protect those who were weak. Hell, that was one of the reasons he was in the line of work he was in. Maybe she wouldn't be so quick to turn him down if he showed them around the hospital. "Just got here. Wanna see?" he asked Shawn.

Shawn glanced back and forth between his sister and Fisher. It was only after Kylee nodded that Shawn followed Fisher into the exam room where the bobcat lay.

"Jake, what can you tell us about the patient?" Fisher asked.

"*Lynx rufus,*" Jake said, listening to the animal's heart with his stethoscope. "His vitals are steady. Bleeding is controlled. Actually pretty minor. Waiting on X-rays."

Fisher nodded. Sounded like everything was on track. He turned to Shawn. "He's out cold, if you want to pet him."

Shawn stared at the bobcat. "Really?"

Fisher nodded. "Sure thing." He looked at Kylee then, figuring he might need to ask her first. But she was just as transfixed by the animal. Something about the look on her face made his chest feel heavy—and warm. "You, too, Kylee." He smiled at the uncertain expression on her face. "Not every day you get to pet one of these. Normally they have too many teeth and claws."

Shawn moved forward slowly, his hands wavering before sinking deep in the cat's fur. "He's so soft." He looked at his sister. *"Kylee."* The boy's exasperated tone brought a smile to Fisher's lips. How often had he goaded Renata into doing something?

Kylee placed Chance's rawhide chew on the counter and moved to Shawn's side. Her fingers barely touched the cat's fur before she drew back. Her hand returned, stroking the bobcat's head with more confidence. "Poor thing," she murmured. The smile that appeared on her face was mesmerizing. She was mesmerizing—too mesmerizing.

Fisher understood the awe on Shawn's face. There was something magical about animals, they inspired delight and wonder—something it was easy to forget when you worked with them day in and day out.

"What happened to it?" Kylee asked. "How did it get hurt? His leg…is it broken?"

"It looks broken," Shawn echoed.

Fisher nodded toward the bobcat's back leg. "Got hit by a Jeep."

Shawn winced.

Fisher nodded.

"How did it get here?" Kylee asked, her brow furrowing.

"The driver, the one who hit him, loaded him into her car while it was knocked out and drove him here." Fisher shrugged, still amazed that the woman hadn't stopped to think about what might happen once the bobcat woke up. A slew of stitches wasn't good, but it could have been a lot worse.

Jake jumped in. "Then the bobcat woke up while she was still in the Jeep."

Kylee's mouth fell open. "Is she okay?"

"She will be. But she needs stitches," Michelle answered, handing the chart to Fisher for review.

Kylee grabbed Shawn by the shoulders and pulled him back.

"He won't be waking up anytime soon," Fisher reassured them. "It's safe, I promise."

Shawn resumed stroking the bobcat, his black hair flopping forward onto his forehead. "He has spots."

"Know why the bobcat is spotted?" Fisher asked, glancing over the notes Jake and Michelle had added to the chart.

"No," Shawn shook his head.

Fisher handed the clipboard back to Michelle. "One Native American tribe, Shawnee I think, say the bobcat trapped a wily rabbit. Once he was caught, the rabbit told the bobcat he'd taste better grilled. So the bobcat built a fire. But the rabbit told the bobcat the best wood to use was damp wood. Know what happens when you burn damp wood?" he asked Shawn.

Shawn shook his head.

"The wood swells, pops and can be a real fire hazard," he explained. "So when the wood burned, it popped and snapped, and the embers singed the cat's fur, leaving spots."

Kylee frowned. "Mean rabbit."

"Smart rabbit." Shawn laughed. "Bet he didn't get eaten."

Fisher chuckled. "I bet you're right." He glanced at Kylee to find her watching him.

"What will happen to him?" she asked.

He swallowed, unnerved by the intensity in her blue eyes. "We'll fix him. If he can be fully rehabilitated, he'll be released in the wild. If not, my brother Archer has a rehabilitation and refuge center. He'll take in any animal that needs a safe place to live out their life." He saw the slight crease between her brows. She looked like that a lot when they were together but he didn't know why. He got the feeling she was waiting for him to do or say something else. He hoped she wouldn't be disappointed to know that, with him, what you saw was what you got.

LISTENING TO FISHER'S folktale filled her with unexpected longing. She didn't put much stock in being sentimental or dwelling on the past. Most of her memories were best forgotten. But she had a few of her mother that she cherished. Climbing into her mother's lap with a book, the feel of her mother's softness, her sweet scent engulfing her and the soft lilt of her voice. Kylee had felt safe and protected…two things she hadn't felt in years, two things she'd almost forgotten were a part of her childhood.

"Dr. Archer on his way?" Fisher asked the students.

"Yes, sir," the girl answered. "He said he'd meet us in the OR after X-rays were done."

"I'm betting there's a hip issue," Fisher spoke, leaning over the bobcat. "See the displacement?" Both the students crowded beside him, peering at the slight bulge of bone along the cat's hip. Kylee almost smiled at their eagerness. "Make sure you get clear images. Might want to have an ultrasound on standby, as well."

Shawn was still stroking the bobcat, but even he'd bent closer to the animal. His eyes narrowed as he studied the area Fisher had pointed out. His nose scrunched up and he frowned as he realized what the lump might mean. "Will you have to do surgery on him?" Shawn asked.

Fisher smiled at her brother. "Looks like it. He'll be up and around in no time."

Kylee was surprised to realize she believed him. And, from the small smile on Shawn's face, so did he.

"Since he's in such capable hands, how about I show you around?" Fisher offered.

"That would be cool." Shawn was instantly excited.

It did sound cool, but she knew Fisher was being polite. "No, we should go," she argued, placing a calming hand on her brother's shoulder. "We don't want to interrupt. You obviously have work to do."

Fisher shook his head. "I wouldn't have offered if it was an interruption. I'm off in—" he glanced at his watch before finishing "—eighteen minutes anyway."

"Please, Kylee," Shawn pleaded. "This place is awesome."

"It really is," the female student agreed. "I came here on a field trip when I was in seventh grade and knew I wanted to go to school here."

"You took a field trip here?" Shawn asked.

"Every year," Fisher said. "The kids get to be a vet for a day."

The girl nodded. "I saw all these dogs and cats and knew this was my future."

Kylee smiled when Shawn looked at her. They hadn't spent much time talking about the future before. Their days had been about surviving—keeping Jesse happy. Thinking beyond their day-to-day was dangerous; it led to ideas and hope. And hope meant there was something to lose. But if they stayed here in Stonewall Crossing that *might* change. Shawn could grow up making plans for a real future, have friends and gain legal skills for a good life.

She didn't say much as Fisher gave them a tour. It was an overwhelming facility, full of high-tech gadgets and impressive equipment. The only experiences she'd had with medical facilities had been for stitches, slings or treatment for her latest injury. She'd always equated hospitals and clinics with the suffering she and Shawn had experienced. But now…she saw beyond the injury to the healing. What would it be like to be a student here? To be trained on the newest, best equipment. To have engaging and passionate teachers like Fisher. To help.

Shawn had a million questions and Fisher answered them all—just like she'd known he would. She was beginning to consider Fisher was something she thought didn't exist: a good guy. She waited for Fisher to be preoccupied with Shawn before studying him. Fisher's smile, his laugh, his easygoing nature was a stark contrast to Jesse. Which was good—Shawn needed a better role model.

"Recovery ward," Fisher said, pushing open another door.

Chance greeted them with several awkward spins and the frantic wave of his stubby tail.

"He's happy to see you," Fisher translated.

"Even I figured that one out." Kylee couldn't stop her smile then. "He looks great."

"He's a real sweetheart." Fisher squatted so he could rub the dog behind his good ear. "Good disposition. A real pleaser."

"What will happen to him when he's all healed?" Shawn asked, sitting on the floor. Chance was on him then, circling Shawn, licking his ear, whimpering with unfiltered happiness. "Hey, boy, I brought you something."

Chance took the rawhide chew, put it in the corner of his cage and ran—awkward but steady—back to Shawn. Shawn held his arms out, hugging the little dog close and carefully rubbing the wiggling creature.

"We'll find him a home," Fisher said, watching Shawn. "He's got too much energy to live here at the school."

"Some animals do?" she asked, surprised.

"Tripod does," Fisher answered, turning his green eyes on her.

"Who's Tripod?" Shawn asked, giggling as Chance curled up in his lap.

"He's a pretty important cat, actually. He comforts the patients that are hurting."

"A cat?" Kylee repeated. "Patients, as in other animals?"

"Not all of 'em. He seems to know who needs him." Fisher grinned. "I know it sounds weird but he helps. I've seen it, calming the other animals' BP. He'll lie by them, groom them, sometimes he just puts his paw on them. He must give off some sort of healing vibe that other animals respond to."

"Sounds like another story?" Shawn asked. "Like the bobcat and his spots?"

Fisher chuckled. "It's true. I promise."

"A nurse cat?" Shawn asked, still skeptical.

"Pretty much," Fisher agreed.

Kylee was intrigued. "That's amazing."

"It is. Even more so considering he's three-legged." Fisher's gaze caught and held hers. It was warm and steady, soothing yet…alarming. "I'll take you back to the offices. He'll be there somewhere," he offered, completely unaware of the conflicting emotions he inspired in her.

"We don't want to keep you." Even if she was a little tempted. "I need to get Shawn back for dinner—"

"After we take Chance for a walk, we could get some burgers?" He was asking her, his gaze never wavering.

She tore her gaze from his and knelt on the ground by Shawn. Having dinner with him would make it a little hard to avoid him and *no men* was still number one on her list. She was still trying to figure Fisher Boone out. What did he want? Why was he so nice? He'd have an angle, men always did. Until she knew what it was she needed to avoid him. She looked at him. "I have to work tonight." Which was true.

He paused, studying her. She didn't like it. She didn't like the disappointed sigh, the slight narrowing of his watchful gaze or the smile that spread slowly across his handsome face. He cocked his head to the side. "I was heading to the bowling alley down the road, meeting up with Jo and Hunter and their son, Eli. You might have met him at Shots? He and Shawn are buddies." Fisher paused. "I could take Shawn. Probably be a bunch more boys their age there. Won't keep him out late. And we can bring you a burger after?"

She frowned at Fisher. He had no right to ask like that—in front of Shawn. Of course, he'd have no way of knowing she rarely let Shawn out of her sight. She had good reason. At least, she'd had good reason when they were in Las Vegas. But they weren't in Las Vegas anymore. And things here, in Stonewall Crossing, were different.

She wavered, but her unease won out. They might not be in Las Vegas, but that didn't mean she was okay sending her little brother off with someone who was practically a stranger.

She glanced at her brother and their gazes locked. He must have understood her hesitation because Shawn murmured, "Thanks anyway, Dr. Fisher." The tone of his voice revealed just how frustrated her little brother was.

"No problem. Maybe next time. Here." Fisher handed her brother the leash. "Let's take Chance out for some exercise."

She watched the dog wiggle and squirm as Shawn attached the leash. Shawn's laugh was infectious, making her smile in spite of the ache in her chest. She hated disappointing Shawn but the years had taught her to protect, not trust. Trust wasn't something she did easily. Everything about Fisher was unknown.

Fisher nodded toward the door at the end of the recovery wing. "Chance knows the way," he said to Shawn.

Kylee watched as her little brother was pulled toward the door by a very excited Chance.

"I'm sorry if I overstepped," Fisher said quietly.

She stared at him. He was apologizing?

"I just thought…" He shrugged. "He and Eli are about the same age. A boy needs friends. And a dog." He nodded after them.

Kylee studied his face. There was no hint of teasing. He *seemed* sincere. It would be so much easier if she could find some way to believe the worst of him. She needed to keep Fisher at arm's length. She knew how to do that. For the last few years it had been her and Shawn against the world. It made life a lot easier. Having friendships? This was foreign territory. She was about to say "I don't know you," but stopped herself. Any explanation would require more information than she was willing to give. Instead she said, "Shawn's had a lot of disappointments in life—"

"I wasn't planning on disappointing him, Kylee. Bowling and burgers and a few laughs. According to my nephew Eli, kids like that sort of thing."

She sucked in a deep breath, turning her attention to Shawn. He had left the door open—so she could see him, flat on his back, with the dog crawling over him. *Kids like that sort of thing.* Shawn's childhood hadn't exactly been easy. Then again, neither had hers.

"Kylee?" Fisher's voice was so soft. "How about we plan for two weeks from today? Me, you, Shawn and my brother and his family?"

She didn't answer.

"I'll warn you," Fisher kept going, "I'm a damn fine bowler."

She tried not to grin. "You have a high opinion of yourself, Doc."

"If the shoe fits." He nudged her, winking.

"You two coming?" Shawn called.

"I'll think about it. And thanks for the offer of a ride, but we'll walk home," she said.

"I don't mind—"

"We'll walk," she insisted. She picked up the pace, putting distance between herself and Fisher. The more distance the better. Yes, Fisher was nice. And handsome. And he had a great sense of humor. If she was being honest with herself, she'd admit there *seemed* to be a lot to like. Which scared her. She didn't have the best judgment when it came to men, and she had the scars to prove it.

Chapter Four

Fisher slid the envelope across the bar. "Don't make a big deal out of this," Fisher warned the grinning old man.

Cutter shook his head, but he kept grinning.

"What?"

"In my day a fella would bring flowers," Cutter muttered. "Or take her out for a nice dinner."

"This is for *Shawn*," Fisher argued. No twelve-year-old boy wanted to spend the whole summer cooped up indoors, not knowing anyone, with nothing to do. "The camp had a last minute cancellation—"

"I get it." Cutter interrupted. "I still say you're takin' the scenic route on this trip. But whatever works."

Fisher couldn't hold back his smile then. "I owe you one, Cutter."

"Good for the boy." Cutter tapped the envelope on the counter. "Kid deserves a break. So does his sister."

Over a very bad cup of coffee, Cutter had shared everything he knew about his new employee and her brother. It wasn't much, but it was enough. Kylee and Shawn were on their own. They had no family and no safety net. Cutter's sister ran a boardinghouse for those who'd otherwise be homeless. She was the one who had packed Kylee and Shawn onto a bus in Las Vegas and sent them to Stonewall Crossing.

The hardest part for Fisher had been hearing the state they were in when they arrived. Hearing that Kylee's arm had been in a sling, her mouth had been full of stitches and Shawn's arms and neck were covered with bruises made him see red. It had been years since he'd wanted to beat the crap out of someone, but he did—badly. If he knew who'd hurt them…well, it was good he didn't.

Cutter leaned on the countertop. "She filled out that job application. For Donna's job, the front desk manager at the vet school? I admit, I wouldn't quit hassling her about it until I'd seen it was done with my own two eyes." Cutter shrugged. "But now she's holding on to the damn thing instead of turning it in. Scared, I think. Not that she'd ever admit to it. She's a feisty one."

Fisher grinned, in full agreement with Cutter's opinion of Kylee and his take on things. Starting over was scary. Someone like Kylee, who was determined to be independent, would resist assistance unless there was no other choice. He admired her, her strength and devotion to her little brother. If there was something he could do to help Kylee and Shawn, he'd do it—without analyzing why he was so willing to do so. Sad as he was to see Donna retire, this would be a real opportunity for Kylee—and Shawn.

"Keep working on her," Fisher offered. "No offense, but it'd be good for both of them."

"Why the hell do you think I suggested she find another job, boy?" Cutter got riled up. "Go on, now, and get yourself outta here. I got things to do."

Fisher left the bar, disappointed. Waylon was tied to

the hitching post out front. "Ready to go?" he asked, patting the horse's neck.

Waylon snorted.

He and Waylon rode into town once in a while. Since Waylon took part in a lot of parades, Fisher liked to keep the horse comfortable around cars and people. Riding in town helped with that. And since Archer had been even more short-tempered than usual this morning, Fisher had saddled up Waylon and headed out. He climbed onto the saddle and turned the horse toward the vet hospital. While Fisher got caught up on charting and checked in on some patients, Waylon could get some extra attention from the students on the large animal rotation.

He'd hoped he'd see Kylee this morning—it had been almost a week since she and Shawn visited the vet school. But since she wasn't around, he decided to stop in at Pop's bakery for some breakfast. His gaze swept the warm peaches and pinks that colored the early-morning sky, the faintest dusting of bright white clouds yellowing with the rise of the sun. It was going to be a gorgeous day.

He whistled, peeking in the storefront windows of the shops on the town square. Sundays were quiet days on Main Street, most shops opened late and closed early. Days like today were meant for tubing the river, barbecues and, according to his father, work around the ranch. He didn't mind the work; he and his family had taken care of their land for generations and he was proud to do it. Maybe after he'd checked in at the hospital and after he'd completed his father's work list, he could talk the family into roasting marshmallows over a big fire that evening. He dismounted and tied Waylon's reins to the railing before pushing the door to the bakery open.

Carl and Lola, the elderly couple who owned Pop's, both greeted him warmly.

"Morning, Fisher." Lola waved. "What brings you into town this morning?"

"Figured I'd have some breakfast before I head to work." He accepted her hug. "How's life been treating you and Carl?"

"Oh, sugar, life's about as good as it gets, I'd say. Well, until Josie and Hunter give us another grandbaby, that is. You can tell them I said that." She smiled.

"I'll do that," Fisher laughed. "Not that it'll hurry things along." Hunter was married to Carl's only child. And Carl and Lola, Carl's second wife, loved Eli, but they were getting impatient to hold some grandbabies in their arms. Since the Boones had twins in their family, Carl and Lola were hoping they'd get two the first time around. But, as far as Fisher knew, Josie and Hunter were still too wrapped up in each other to be thinking about babies—yet.

"Can't hurt." Lola patted his hand. "What can I get you?"

"Couple of sausage rolls and one raspberry kolache," he paused, glancing at the whiteboard with their specials written on it. "Make that blueberry. And lots of coffee."

"That all?" she asked. "A man as big as you? That's not gonna last you till ten."

Fisher arched a brow at her. "Trying to fatten me up, Lola?"

She laughed, the little bell over the door interrupting them.

George Carson came in, saw Fisher and froze.

Fisher had a choice to make. It was clear the man knew he was in the wrong. But pride was going to stop him from saying as much. Fisher could either stay pissed that Carson lost control or he could do his best to act like it never happened. And damn if he didn't know what holding on to anger could do to a man's soul. He drew in a deep breath and nodded at the man. "Carson."

"Boone." Carson returned the nod and headed to the counter.

"Morning, George." Lola chatted away, taking the other man's order.

Fisher made his way to one of the two tables that were empty, nodding and saying good morning to the rest of the bakery patrons as he went. He'd just taken his seat when the bell over the door rang and his brother Archer arrived.

"Shit," Fisher muttered, shooting a quick glance at Carson.

Luckily, Archer saw Fisher first and headed his way. Archer sat without saying a word, pulling out the newspaper he'd tucked into his bag and spreading it open on the table.

"Good morning to you, too," Fisher murmured. He loved his brother, but a man needed his space. Archer didn't seem to get that. Or, if he did, he didn't care. But then Archer had always been the sort to do what he wanted, when he wanted, regardless of who else might have an opinion or say-so.

He saw Kylee and Shawn before they came in. Shawn was staring at Waylon, tugging on Kylee's arm until she stopped. Neither one of them made a move to touch his horse, but they both took their time looking the horse over. Shawn pulled his sketch pad from the worn backpack he always carried, but Kylee tugged him toward the door. Shawn followed reluctantly.

The bell rang again as they came in. It didn't matter that she wore a T-shirt two sizes too big or that her jeans were so faded one knee was threadbare and in need of patching. Her neck arched as she listened to Shawn, her long black ponytail swinging with each step. She gave Shawn one of her sweet smiles and lovingly squeezed her brother's shoulder. Everything about her mesmerized Fisher.

He swallowed, turning his focus on a safer target—Shawn. The boy kept looking at Waylon, visible through the huge picture windows that lined the front of the bakery. He was pleased to see the letter he'd left with Cutter moments before sticking out of Shawn's back pocket.

Would Shawn want to go? He knew the boy liked horses. He remembered Shawn's sketches, and his reaction to Waylon spoke volumes. Would Kylee let him? He hoped so; it would be good for both of them. Chances were she was going to need some convincing. Her gaze swept the room—making sure it was safe? When her eyes met his, she paused, wavering. Interesting.

He smiled at her, wishing he knew what was going on inside that pretty little head of hers. "Whatever I say," Fisher mumbled to his brother, "I need you to go along with it."

Archer frowned, looking up from his newspaper. "What?"

"Just do it, Archer," Fisher growled as Shawn pulled Kylee toward them. "Morning."

Kylee's smile was small, but it was a start. "Morning."

"Hey, Dr. Boone and Dr. Boone." Shawn shook his head. "That's weird."

"You're tellin' me. How about I'm just Fisher and he's Dr. Archer?" Fisher laughed. "Join us?"

"Oh, I—" Kylee's gaze bounced back and forth between them.

Archer frowned. It took everything Fisher had not to kick his brother under the table.

Kylee started to back away. "No, we can't—"

"Sure, you can." Fisher nodded, nudging Archer's foot under the table.

"Yes," Archer said. "Sit. Please."

Fisher sighed. "You'll have to excuse my brother. He's much better with animals."

Kylee smiled, he saw it—and it warmed him through.

Shawn sat, pulling the letter from his pocket and placing it on the table.

Fisher gratefully accepted the cup of coffee Lola set on the table in front of him. "Needed this, thank you, Lola."

"I don't know if someone's told you, and I hesitated to mention it before, but you've got a black eye, Fisher." Lola patted him on the shoulder, causing everyone at the table to laugh.

"I do?" Fisher feigned surprise. "No wonder it's sore."

"You should have seen it a week ago," Shawn chimed in.

"That bad, huh?" Lola asked.

Shawn made a face. Which made everyone laugh again. Even Kylee, though she tried like hell not to.

Eventually, Lola asked, "What can I get everyone this morning? The cinnamon rolls and blueberry kolaches are fresh. All the other specials are on the board."

That was when Kylee saw George Carson. Fisher watched as her blue eyes went round and her body stiffened. Her gaze darted to Shawn, then Fisher, then to Carson. She wanted to leave, every muscle in her body was coiled tight and ready to run. Did she think he'd start something with Carson? Or was she worried about Carson being the instigator? Either way, he should reassure her that everything was all right.

Kylee wasn't the only one who saw Carson. "When did he get here?" Archer snapped. "Did he apologize?"

Fisher shook his head. "Water under the bridge, Archer."

"Maybe for you." His brother's voice was hard.

Fisher smiled then. His brother was thinking about Carson's work ethic and the jeopardy he'd put Archer's horses in. Not the fact that he'd treated his brother like a punching bag. "If I'm okay with the man getting his breakfast, I think you should be, too."

Kylee frowned at Archer—and it warmed Fisher's heart. He winked at her, wincing as it pulled against his healing cut. She winced, too, making him smile. She shook her head then.

"What?" Fisher asked her.

She looked at him, a long assessing look, before answering, "I'm still adjusting to the norm here in Stonewall Crossing."

"I like it," Shawn piped up.

"I do, too," Fisher agreed.

Archer sat stoically while George Carson left, carrying a large pastry box with him. He did notice Kylee's posture relax once the door closed behind Carson's back.

"Have you lived here your whole life?" Shawn asked.

"Most of it," Fisher said. "Went away for a few years for college, served in the reserves—canine corps unit, of course—but that's it."

"Where'd you go for school?" Shawn asked. "Travel with the reserves?"

"You ask a lot of questions," Archer commented.

All eyes turned on Archer.

"That's not bad," Archer clarified. "It's a sign of intelligence."

Shawn nodded. "Oh."

"He was in gifted and talented classes when we…at his last school," Kylee nodded. "He gets bored easily."

Archer nodded. "Need to keep him busy."

Archer's words had Kylee stiffening and Fisher's protective instincts on the rise. Archer hadn't meant to sound critical, he just did—that's the way he always sounded. But Kylee didn't know that so she might take Archer's comment personally. In the time he'd spent with her, he'd learned one thing for certain. Kylee was doing the best she could for Shawn—she always would.

Fisher glanced at the letter on the table, the one Shawn kept glancing at. "What's that?"

Shawn offered it to him, leaning back so Lola could serve them their breakfasts. "Thank you, ma'am," Shawn said to Lola, before turning back to Fisher. "A camp. Kylee doesn't want me to go—"

"I didn't say that, Shawn." Kylee sighed. "It's just…it has to cost something or have some sort of catch or condition or something." Her blue eyes searched his, curious.

Fisher's heart hurt for her. He and Renata had puzzled over every word of the letter. Instinct told him Kylee would throw the letter away if it came across as a pity offer.

"What camp?" Archer asked.

"Horse camp," Shawn offered, taking a big bite of his blueberry roll.

"Do you have any interest in horses?" Archer asked.

"He draws them all the time," Kylee said.

"He's good, too," Fisher said. "If you have any new ones, I'd like to see them."

Shawn nodded. "Okay." He pulled his battered sketchbook out and offered it to Fisher. "They're my favorite animal. I've never seen one up close before..." He glanced out the window. "Until now... But I've read a lot about them. Did you know the horse has the largest eye out of all land animals? You probably did, since you're a veterinarian." Shawn grinned.

"Land *mammals*," Archer clarified, but Fisher could tell his brother's interest was piqued. "Do you want to go?"

"Yes." Shawn's answer was almost apologetic.

"Is it far?" Archer asked.

Shawn shook his head. "I don't know. Is Boone Ranch far?"

Fisher felt Archer's eyes on him, but didn't acknowledge it. Archer knew the camp was full, that it was far from free, *and* there was a waiting list. He could deal with Archer's interrogation later. Right now, he wanted Shawn to have some fun this summer. He didn't resist as Archer took the letter from him, reading over it.

But Fisher had a hard time meeting Kylee's gaze when she asked, "Why Shawn?"

Because he wanted to do something nice for them? He wanted to give the boy a real childhood experience? Somehow he suspected she'd find that an unacceptable answer so he said, "Maybe Cutter nominated him?" and hoped she'd take the bait.

"Cutter?" It was hard to miss the skepticism in her tone.

He nodded, her assessing gaze slightly unnerving.

"This is entirely our sister Renata's program so I can't

say a word on this scholarship process," Archer offered. "But Cutter's involvement does make the most sense."

Fisher hoped she'd accept his brother's argument. It did sound logical.

"He's already done so much for us." She glanced at Shawn. "Too much."

"What's the harm in him going?" Archer handed the letter back to Kylee. "From the sounds of that, it's all taken care of. My sister works hard on this all year. Kids come from all over to go. Shawn would enjoy it."

Fisher smiled at his brother, pleased by his support. Archer didn't smile back. Fisher sighed.

Archer flipped through Shawn's sketchbook, taking his time with each sketch.

"I won't go if you say no," Shawn said to his sister. "If you're worried that Jesse's going to find us—"

"Shawn," she interrupted quickly. Her skin had paled and her hands were shaking. "Let me call them first, okay? Just to make sure." Her voice was high, pinched.

Who was Jesse? Were they hiding from him? Were they in danger? He thought about what Cutter had told him this morning. One look at Shawn spoke volumes. But getting angry wouldn't help them and that's what he wanted to do. "Want me to call my sister?" Fisher offered. "Since she's the one in charge."

Archer shot him a look that he pointedly ignored.

Kylee poked at her cinnamon roll. "I can call."

"Sure," he relented, wishing he could say or do something to lighten the mood. Whoever this Jesse was, he'd done enough damage. They were here now, safe—Fisher would make sure of that.

"You should call her," Archer's words surprised him.

"Get all your questions answered. I don't blame you for being skeptical."

Fisher bit back a grin. Archer was right. The best way to ease doubts was to answer questions. And he wanted Kylee to feel good about this. He didn't need to worry. It was all Renata's idea. When one of their out-of-state students had canceled at the last minute Renata had been the one to think of Shawn first. Since her "baby brother" was "sweet on Kylee" she wanted to help however she could. Fisher had offered to pay Shawn's tuition as an anonymous scholarship and Renata had typed up the letter. Now all he had to do was make sure Shawn actually went.

"How's Chance?" Shawn asked. "We wanted to come see him, but Cutter's been too busy to drive us."

"Better every day." Fisher was considering adopting Chance for himself. The dog was smart, smart enough to learn how to work with cattle—even with his bum leg. Chance would be a good companion...once Archer was back under his own roof. "I've got some kittens to feed at the clinic this morning. Kylee, would you and Shawn be free to help out? We're always in need of volunteers."

"Kittens?" Shawn asked.

"They came in last night, late. Apparently the mom was hit in a parking lot and an old woman brought in the kittens," Fisher explained.

"That was kind." Kylee spoke softly, still considering her cinnamon roll. He liked the hint of a smile on her mouth.

"Can we, Kylee?" Shawn polished off his roll. "I'll volunteer."

Kylee glanced at Fisher, her posture easing a little. "I guess."

"I'm sure the little guys'll be happy to see you." Fisher

knew *he* was. Now he just needed to convince Archer to ride Waylon so he could drive them to the hospital. And he'd need to convince Waylon to let Archer ride him.

KYLEE WIPED DOWN the counter that ran along the back of the dance hall. Friday nights were becoming her favorite. Seeing all the families together, generations gathered together for fun and camaraderie, gave her a glimpse of what life should be. She had no illusions about *her* future—but there was hope for Shawn. A word she didn't have a lot of experience with.

Shawn waved from his seat at the end of the bar, his sketchbook and pencils in front of him. He'd wandered some, enjoying the company of a few boys close to his age. But not for long. Being social was a challenge, even a little stressful. She understood all too well. Her job required her to interact with people but it was all superficial and limited. Making friends, having conversations, was different. Was it possible he'd forget? That eventually he wouldn't be so restrained or hesitant? She wanted that for him. She wanted him to smile, laugh, to act like a kid.

Since it was Friday, Shawn wasn't banished to the break room or the apartment. Cutter believed the dance hall was for families, not just adults.

"Need anything?" she asked, giving him a one-armed hug.

"A soda?" Shawn asked.

"What are you working on?" she asked, sliding a glass of water across the counter.

He frowned at the water, but emptied the glass. "Nothing much."

He'd moved his arm to shield his sketch, but she'd

glimpsed what looked like a kitten. "You know, you can put that away and hang out with Eli."

"Later, maybe. Need me to move? Am I in the way?"

She covered his hand with hers. "No. You're great."

He grinned at her.

"Sorry if I'm being nosy or overprotective. Old habits die hard." She shook her head. "I'm trying to lighten up." She nodded at a girl who had been staring at her brother. "You know, you could try dancing."

Shawn glanced at the girl, then back at his sister. "Nope." He shook his head. "I'm good."

"Hey, pretty lady." A man rested his elbow on the counter. "Any chance you can get a pitcher for me and my friends over there?" He nodded at the table behind him.

"Coming up," she answered, giving Shawn a little farewell salute. She grabbed an empty plastic pitcher and turned to the tap.

"That's some view," the man murmured.

She ignored the urge to pull her shirt over her butt and kept working.

He tried again. "Don't remember seein' you here before. And with a *face* like yours, I'd remember." There was a brief pause before he asked, "How about you join us when you get your break?"

She ignored him, finished filling the pitcher and placed it on the counter. "Fifteen dollars."

"You keep the change." He placed a twenty on the counter. "You decide you're lookin' for a little fun, come on over and visit with a couple of real cowboys. What d'ya think?"

She shot him a look then. He was somewhat attractive, fit and trim, but his smile was oily and his interest in her boobs was a little too obvious. He seemed to be waiting for her answer. Was he serious? Did women really respond to this?

"Limited time offer." His gaze swept over her face before settling on her chest again. "Just in town for the rodeo tomorrow night. Be a real shame for you to miss out on a once-in-a-lifetime experience."

She tried not to smile. She'd had a lot of bad pick-up lines thrown her way. But the whole "once-in-a-lifetime experience" was a new one.

"Come on, darlin', give me a smile," the man continued. "Sure would be nice to show me some Southern hospitality."

Fine. If it would make him shut up and leave her alone…

She smiled at him, before resuming her normal blank expression. Over the years, she'd learned the best way to handle flirty guys was with as little reaction as possible. He seemed harmless enough, just oblivious.

"That's a start," the man said. "How about a little more…enthusiasm?"

She shrugged. "That's about as enthusiastic or hospitable as I get."

"Can I get a couple of pitchers?" a woman's voice interrupted.

"Enjoy your night," Kylee murmured before heading down the bar to the woman waiting. Kylee had seen her before—with Fisher. The woman had to be a Boone—she looked too much like Fisher not to be. "Two pitchers?" Kylee asked.

The woman just smiled at her. "Hi. I'm Renata Boone," the woman said, holding out her hand. "Fisher's my twin. Fraternal, of course. It's really nice to meet you."

"You, too." Kylee shook hands with the woman. "Kylee James. Two pitchers?"

"No rush. I was mostly trying to get rid of Mr. Belt Buckle over there. I was worried he was going to go for your boobs any second there, the way he was staring at them," Renata said, sliding onto the bar stool.

Kylee couldn't stop her laugh, she was too surprised. "Mr. Belt Buckle?" she asked when she'd recovered.

"Think he's overcompensating?" Renata nodded at the table where the cowboys sat. "Look at the size of that thing."

"Um, I'd rather not. Don't want him to get the wrong impression." Kylee wrinkled her nose.

"Oh, right, good call. Then he'd start the boob staring again," Renata agreed. "So, what do you think of Stonewall Crossing?"

Kylee glanced at Fisher's twin; she could see a lot of similarities. The green eyes, the easy smile, the lively conversation. She liked Renata instantly. "It's a nice town."

"Isn't it?" Renata smiled. "Fisher said you're from Las Vegas so this must be a change."

"He did?" Fisher had mentioned her? How did he know she and Shawn had come from Las Vegas? She was careful who she shared private details with.

"Not too small for you? Or too quiet?" Renata asked, watching her closely.

"I like the small and the quiet." Kylee shrugged, her gaze sweeping the room before she admitted, "Honestly, there are times I do feel a little out of place."

"We need to fix that." Renata shook her head. "I hope you got the scholarship letter for Shawn's camp tuition. I hear he loves horses and that's what camp is all about. Learning how to take care of them, ride them and a little bit of everyday, hands-on know-how."

"He wants to go," Kylee said. "I was worried there might be more to it? A fee or deposit?"

Renata shook her head. "Nope. He just has to get there and home, we'll take care of the rest."

Renata's words made Kylee uneasy, but she didn't have too long to dwell on things because Fisher arrived. She didn't turn her head or acknowledge his presence, but she knew he was there—just out of her peripheral vision.

Fisher's voice washed over her, warm and oddly comforting. "Hey bartender-lady," he called out. "Is this woman harassing you?"

She bit back a smile as she turned to face him. "Doc."

"I am not harassing her," Renata argued. "Since no one introduced me, I decided it was high time to meet the girl you keep talking about."

Keep talking about? She looked at Fisher, but he was leaning against the bar without a care in the world. "Can I get a bottle, please?" He glanced her way, smiling. "And thank you."

She popped the top of his beer of choice and placed it on the counter. But his attention had shifted to the table where Mr. Belt Buckle and his friends sat. Everything about him changed. His posture was tense, his expression was hard, his jaw rigid and eyes intent. She followed his gaze, shaking her head when Mr. Belt Buckle and his friends raised their glasses of beer at her. "Friend of yours?" she asked.

"No." He turned back to her, his gaze a little too intent. "Busy night?"

She nodded.

"It's like two full-time jobs," Renata jumped in. "The bartending part and the warding off sleazy guys looking for a hookup. Not that I'm talking about you, brother of mine." She smiled sweetly.

Kylee laughed again, then shrugged. "It's part of the job. Believe me, Mr. Belt Buckle wasn't a problem."

"Guess things are a little rougher in Las Vegas?" Renata asked.

Kylee nodded. Rougher was an understatement. She'd learned how to fend off the more aggressive ones, physically if she had to. But it had been just as hard when she wasn't working. The one time she'd stood up to Jesse, told him they wouldn't work for him anymore, he'd kicked them out—onto the street.

What followed were days of hiding. Nights of bitter cold. And hunger so strong she hurt. She'd fed Shawn out of a dumpster more than a handful of times...before she'd gone back to Jesse and begged him to take them back.

Jesse had found the three of them a room in Miss Millie's boardinghouse, but it wasn't much better. The more drugs Jesse used, the more unpredictable he was. She and Shawn knew fear, fear of the unknown. Jesse was going to expect payment for taking them back...

She shook off the memories to find Fisher and Renata staring at her. "Sorry. What did you say?" she asked awkwardly.

"Thank you." Renata's gaze was thoughtful and assessing, but kind. "I'll get these back to the table," she murmured, carrying the two pitchers to the table the Boones inhabited across the dance hall.

"You okay?" Fisher asked, setting his beer bottle on the bar. "That jackass cowboy say something to upset you? Need me to chase him off?"

Kylee looked at Fisher, really looked at him. His gaze was so focused she felt lost. The longer he stared, the more off center she became. It unnerved her to see his concern for her well-being. Like he really cared about her...like she mattered to him.

She swallowed, holding on to the bar with both hands for support. He *didn't* care about her, he didn't *know* her. Why would he try to protect her? Didn't he know she didn't need protecting? She drew in a deep breath and said, "No. I'm fine. He didn't do or say anything wrong. He was just being...friendly."

Fisher's brow furrowed deeply. "Not too friendly?"

Kylee shook her head. "Doc, I can take care of myself."

"I didn't say you couldn't, Kylee." He let out a slow breath, his eyes searching hers. "I'm just saying you don't have to. There are other people here looking out for you, too." He tilted his beer bottle in salute.

The thumping of her heart drowned out everything else. Jesse had said he'd look out for them. He'd made big promises, then left big injuries. But she was beginning to believe Fisher Boone was the kind of man who would honor his word, protect his family, and take care of those he cared about. The kind of man she wanted Shawn to grow into. The kind of man she'd dreamed of finding—but would never deserve to have.

Chapter Five

"It's a closet," Kylee argued.

"We don't have anything to put in it," Shawn argued. "So why can't I use it as a bedroom?" She and Shawn hadn't collected much stuff over the years. If it couldn't fit into one of their backpacks, they didn't need it.

Kylee peered into the closet. It was a decent size, she supposed. And there was a small window in the top. Why there was a window in the closet, she didn't know. A clothes rod ran along the length of it, but there were no hangers or garments stored here. All of their clothes fit inside the large chest of drawers in the main room.

"It is a closet." Shawn agreed. "Or it could be my room."

Kylee wiped at the smudge of paint on his forehead. They'd spent most of the day painting the dark wood paneled walls a nice yellow-buttercream color—the only color on the discounted paint shelf that she and Shawn had agreed upon. Their little studio had gone from dark and dingy to—almost—light and airy. She turned, assessing the work they'd done. The apartment was clean but bare.

At one end of the apartment was a wall of cabinets, a stove and a banged-up white refrigerator that hummed loudly but kept things cold. The only furnishings in their apartment had been there when they moved in. There was a worn, but comfortable, leather sectional with a reclining end chair that Kylee slept on each night. The large chest of drawers and double bed were behind the sectional, wedged into a corner. Shawn slept in this makeshift bedroom…and now he wanted to sleep in the closet.

"What will you sleep on?" she asked.

"I don't need to sleep on anything."

"You're not sleeping on the floor." Kylee sighed. Shawn didn't complain. Not about their regular diet of ramen noodles, peanut butter crackers and cereal. He never said a thing about needing new clothes or the hole in his shoe, being left alone while she worked, the odd hours they kept or being lonely. Now he wanted his own room—even if it was a closet. Why not? "You can sleep here—"

Shawn did a fist pump and called out, *"Yes!"*

"But not until we get you something to sleep on. We'll look at the rummage sale," she finished, watching his enthusiasm deflate. "And we should see about getting you a fan in there so you don't get overheated." She peered inside. "There's no air in here."

Shawn laughed. "No air? Guess we've come a long way from when we were with Jesse…" He broke off, shrugging. She knew he was imagining some of the places they'd slept and lived. She was, too.

And she hugged him close as he said, "Things have changed. For the better."

She nodded. "I agree." She glanced at the clock and released him. "But we better hurry or we won't have time to go to the rummage sale before I have to go to work.

You need a shower," she teased, poking several dots along his nose and cheek.

"You do, too." He grinned.

She glanced down at her white shirt, which was spattered with paint. So were her arms and chest.

"It's in your hair, too," he offered up.

"Great." She pulled one of her two pairs of jeans from the chest of drawers along with a black T-shirt. She held it up, frowning at how thin the fabric was getting. The seam under the arm looked ready to give at any moment.

"You need clothes," Shawn offered. "They sell clothes at rummage sales?"

Kylee shrugged. "I'm not really sure what we'll find. Guess we'll find out together."

Twenty minutes later she and Shawn walked across the town square to the community center parking lot. She tried not to get caught up in the panic that the crowd stirred. She tried not to assess who'd be best to bump into in order to steal their wallets or—if Jesse had someone casing the cars—car keys. She'd been pretty good at it, her hands were small and she was fast. Shawn was better. Her chest hurt at the memory of his smile when he brought home a sack full of wallets from walking the Strip. But that was the past.

The parking lot was covered in canopies, the small tents spilling onto two empty adjoining lots. Tables were crammed close together, covered with everything from dishes to linens, shoes to books. Kylee thought about the money in her pocket. Not much, but just enough.

She let Shawn wander, making him promise he'd keep his hands to himself and only tell her if there was something he really needed. He knew the difference between need and want.

Kylee paused by a clothing rack, fingering the light-weight fabric of a filmy blue blouse between her thumb and forefinger. It was soft, silky and completely impractical.

"Hey, Kylee." Renata peeked over the top of the rack. "Nice day for shopping."

Kylee nodded. The summer sun was hot, but there was a refreshing breeze that made the temperature bearable. "Hi, Renata." If Renata was here, maybe some of the other Boones were, too. Namely, Fisher. She'd dreamed about him. Dreams so vivid she'd expected him to be beside her when she opened her eyes. His words replayed when she least expected it. Was he looking out for her? Because even though she knew it shouldn't matter, it did.

She glanced around, nervous and excited, searching. If he was here, she'd spot him—head and shoulders above the rest.

"Looking for someone?" Renata asked.

Kylee felt her cheeks go hot. "No...nobody." Why was she looking for Fisher?

Renata nodded, smiling. "So, what are we shopping for? Anything you buy at our booth goes to help the women's shelter." Renata took the shirt Kylee had been admiring and held it up to her. "You'd look nice in this. The blue does awesome things for your eyes. And it's pretty," Renata continued. "A girl needs something pretty now and then."

Kylee couldn't think of a single thing to say about that. It would be nice to feel pretty. It would be nice for Fisher to think she looked pretty...

She swallowed, firmly shoving aside that train of thought. She didn't *need* anything pretty. She needed a couple of shirts and maybe another pair of jeans. Shawn needed that plus some.

"No?" Renata asked.

Kylee shook her head. "It is pretty but I need clothes for work." She pointed at her shirt. "Practical work clothes."

Renata cocked her head, nodding. "Follow me," she said, leading her through a row of racks and into the booth. A tall blonde girl was hanging more shirts on the rack. She smiled at Kylee as Renata made introductions, "Kylee, this is my cousin Tandy. Tandy, this is Kylee."

"Oh, I know who she is." Tandy grinned.

"Hi," Kylee mumbled, catching the grin between the cousins.

"Tandy's new in town, too, sort of. She's visited before but now she's officially a Texan. She's from Montana— my dad's sisters all live there." Renata chatted, flipping through shirts.

"All?" Kylee asked.

"Four," Tandy answered. "We Boones tend to have large families. I mean, we as in the family. Not we as in me." Tandy shook her head. "Have yet to find a fella that can keep up with me."

Renata giggled. "She's going to be working at the vet hospital with my brothers, in the open vet tech position they've had such trouble filling. Now all they need is to find someone to take over the front desk so Donna can retire." Renata paused, holding up a T-shirt. "This."

So the job was still open. And her application was still at home. She didn't have the skills or the experience to be a serious candidate. But…it was still open so maybe she should think about it. The benefits alone made it worth considering. But there were other perks. Like

Fisher. *Where the hell did that come from?* She forced herself to focus, inspecting the black rhinestone-laden T-shirt with an arched brow.

"It's a T-shirt, but it's a little something more." Renata smiled. "Like I said, something pretty now and then. This whole rack is four shirts for five dollars."

Kylee looked at the shirt again. It *was* pretty—and affordable. It had a V neck and curlicue details…and didn't look like it would swallow her up. Might be a nice change from the faded, solid-color men's shirts she'd accrued over the years. She stood silently, watching Renata pull five more out for her inspection.

"These would all look great on you." Renata held them up one at a time. Kylee reluctantly agreed to the black one, a pink one, and a long-sleeved red top with black patches on the elbows and a black pocket on the chest.

"Oh, and this one," Tandy gushed, pulling a bright teal shirt covered in delicate lace and peacock-feather stitching.

"All this for five dollars?" Kylee asked.

Renata nodded. "They're not new and they were donated for a good cause."

Kylee looked at the shirts again. They looked new to her. Since her wardrobe consisted of oversize men's clothing, this was a big departure from her norm.

"What about pants?" Tandy asked. "It's hard to tell under that shirt, but I'm betting you've got a teeny-tiny waist." She turned toward another rack with jeans—all shades and styles.

The total cost for a pair of boots, four shirts and two pairs of jeans was twenty-five dollars. It had been so long since she'd spent money on herself, she almost argued and gave it all back. She could make do with what she had for now. But Renata's reminder that proceeds went to the women's shelter changed her mind. It was the least she could do to support something so worthwhile.

She'd gone to the women's shelter in Vegas one time. Jesse had disappeared, leaving them without food or shelter. By the time Kylee had found the shelter, they'd gone several days without eating. They'd stayed two nights before Jesse found them and brought them home to the hotel room he was currently living in. Jesse had been furious, pushing her around and yelling at her for taking such risks. He told her they'd separate her and Shawn—maybe even try to put him into foster care. She'd believed him, terrified and guilt-ridden about what could have been.

It was Cutter's sister, Miss Millie, who had set her straight. Miss Millie wasn't scared of Jesse the way most people were. She'd tried to take Kylee and Shawn back to the shelter when Jesse was abusive, assuring Kylee it was the safest place in the city for them. But by then Kylee knew they'd never be safe from Jesse. Not as long as they'd stayed in Las Vegas.

"Did Cutter mention dinner on Monday?" Renata asked, pulling Kylee from memories she wished she could erase. "Friends and family. We really hope you'll come, too. Meet some people—we Boones know everyone."

Family meant Fisher…and her heart thumped a little faster. His absence at the bar this week had been all too obvious. No teasing, easy smiles or intense green eyes following her—except in her dreams. It was for the best, him staying away. Accepting the dinner invitation wasn't a good idea. Life might be easier now but, after everything she'd been through, she'd be a fool to let her guard down and start daydreaming about things that would never be.

Renata took the folded items from Tandy and placed them in a large plastic bag, still chattering away. "With Shawn, of course, Eli just loves him. They're going to have lots of fun at camp."

First the camp, now dinner? "I'm still not sure about camp," Kylie spoke up then.

"I thought I was going," Shawn's voice drew all eyes. "I hoped... Never mind." He stared at the ground, kicking a loose pebble with the toe of his worn shoe.

She was being ridiculous. Her resistance came from fear. Fear of losing control, of being reliant on someone else. But she didn't want to live in fear anymore. Not for herself. Not for Shawn.

This wasn't Las Vegas; this was Stonewall Crossing. There was nothing to fear here. That included the people and the Boones. Fisher—all of the Boones—had been nothing but nice to them both. Maybe people did nice things without expecting something in return. Miss Millie had. She'd sent them to Cutter and Stonewall Crossing to help them have a better life. A fresh start. And if she and Shawn were really starting over, she had to give things a chance—for Shawn. That included this amazing opportunity. It was hard to force the words out but she did. "I... I'm sorry, Shawn. You're going. You're going to camp and you're going to have fun."

"Really, Kylee?" Shawn looked at her with wide eyes. "Thank you."

"Don't thank me, Shawn. This is all Miss Boone's idea—"

"Thank you, Miss Boone," Shawn said, shaking Renata's hand. "I mean it. I'm really excited. I'll behave. You won't even know I'm there."

Shawn's words made her heartsick. It was time for

Shawn to be a kid: loud, laughing and full of energy. No, it was long overdue. Things like this camp would help with that. She had to be more careful; Shawn was an intuitive kid. She didn't want her deep-seated worries to rob him of enjoying things. She was truly thankful Renata Boone had given Shawn this opportunity. She needed to act like it.

Renata was looking at her little brother with a perplexed smile. "Oh, no, Shawn, we want to know you're there," Renata assured him. "You just concentrate on having a good time and making friends, okay?"

Shawn nodded, still grinning ear to ear.

"I hope you'll think about dinner, too, Kylee."

Tandy joined in then. "Monday night—should be lots of fun. Uncle Teddy's going to make his famous slow-cooked brisket and you don't want to miss that, trust me."

"The bar is closed Mondays," Shawn offered up, unknowingly removing the only excuse Kylee could have offered to avoid their invitation.

Renata smiled. "Eli will be thrilled."

"He's not the only one," Tandy added, so softly that Kylee wondered if she'd imagined it.

"Can you tell Dr. Fisher I said hello?" Shawn asked.

"Of course." Renata nodded. "He mentioned the three of you bowling soon. Ever bowled before?"

"No, ma'am. Is it hard?" Shawn asked.

"I'm sure Fisher will have you bowling like a pro in no time. He's really good," Tandy offered.

He'd mentioned taking them bowling? To his family? Why? And why did it make her so…happy? She tried not to be. She tried not to think about Fisher's laugh or the way the corners of his eyes crinkled when he smiled.

And his smile—her heart thudded. She swallowed. She didn't want her heart reacting to any man.

"Dr. Fisher's good at everything, isn't he?" Shawn asked.

"Don't let him hear you say that," Renata said with a laugh. "He's already got a big head on his shoulders."

"Well, they are pretty big shoulders," Tandy added.

Yes, they were. Big, broad and powerful. With one punch, he'd put George Carson out. And yet she knew he was just as capable of kindness—she'd seen it in his eyes on more than one occasion. Green eyes that always seemed to find her...and really *see* her. Her heart thudded again, sending a shudder through her chest.

"What else are you looking for?" Renata asked, startling her.

She glanced at Renata, all too aware of the way the woman was watching her. It was a friendly look, one that put Kylee at ease. "Clothes for him," Kylee nodded at Shawn. "And shoes." Then she had to get ready for work.

Renata pointed out the best booths for boys' attire and footwear. "It was nice chatting with you both. Hope to see you Monday," Renata said, waving them off.

"What are you thinking?" Kylee asked as they walked away.

"About camp. And Eli. And dinner at the Boones' place." Shawn paused. "I like Dr. Fisher, too, Kylee. Think I'd be a good veterinarian? And the hospital." Shawn shrugged. "Sometimes all this feels like a dream. I'll wake up and it'll be gone." He glanced at her. "That would suck. A lot."

Kylee nodded.

"Can we volunteer again?" Shawn asked. "At the hospital, I mean. Did you turn in your application for that job yet?"

She paused. "You want me to?"

Shawn looked at her like she was crazy. "Yes. Definitely. I want to be a volunteer, too."

Kylee nodded, but didn't say anything. They'd had a lot of fun feeding the kittens—even if Fisher had been called into an emergency surgery as soon as they'd arrived. Cutter had ended up coming to take them home, but that hadn't deterred Shawn's hero worship one bit. Nope, her little brother thought Fisher was the coolest guy ever. So far, Kylee couldn't disagree.

In no time, Shawn had three pairs of jeans, some shorts, swim trunks, six shirts, tennis shoes and a pair of worn but good-quality cowboy boots. At sixty-eight dollars, they'd done well. But it was still hard to hand over the money.

They headed slowly back through the tables, lingering over odds and ends, laughing out loud over a strange miniature of a gnome riding a turtle. "We should buy that," Shawn giggled. "For the apartment."

Kylee shook her head, still giggling.

But when Shawn paused at a booth full of books, Kylee went back for it. She loved to hear her little brother laugh. She paid quickly, keeping her eye on her brother and shoving the little statue among her newly acquired clothing before returning to his side. "Find something?"

He jumped, so engrossed in the book that he hadn't heard her approach. "Yeah. This kid's going to become a warrior to defeat an invading alien race." He held up the book. "Guess it's a series." He nodded at the box with three more books inside.

The dollar sticker read Award-Winning Children's

Literature on it so Kylee said, "We'll get the series, but you have to write a book report on each of them for me, okay?"

Shawn's eyes went round.

"*If* you agree to the book report?"

He nodded. "Yeah, sure."

Their final purchases included an army cot, a sleeping bag and a small oscillating fan. Kylee knew she'd spent too much money. But Shawn's excitement over having his own room made it all worth it. For the first time in a long time, she felt…safe.

FISHER BROUGHT HIS new surgical resident, Brook Marcus, to Shots. It was one of the best places to meet locals— and Kylee would be there. He'd played two games of pool and danced with half of the elderly widow's group that had come to hear the live country band, but there was still no sign of Kylee. It had been a long week made longer by missing her. And Shawn, too. He was curious to see what pictures the boy had added to his sketchbook.

A quick glance at the bar assured him nothing had changed. Devon's silver-and-brown braid was a familiar sight behind the bar; she'd been working at Shots as long as Fisher could remember. She wiped the bar down while chatting with the patrons seated on the stools, handling the relatively slow Friday night with no trouble.

"Who are you looking for?" Brook asked.

"No one," Fisher replied, shifting the pool cue from one hand to the next.

"Maybe she's not working tonight," Jarvis offered, clearly amused.

Fisher shot Jarvis a look, silencing his friend.

"She who?" Brook asked. "Oh, a lady love?"

He focused on the pool table, setting up his next shot.

"His would-be lady love," Jarvis offered up.

"Details," Brook demanded. Fisher had been a little thrown off by Brook's forthright manner—in everything. It was a benefit in surgery or while handling emergencies, but it could be pretty damn abrupt in average daily conversation.

"Nothing to tell," his cousin Toben said with a laugh. He stood on the opposite side of the table, pool cue in hand. "Fisher's in the friend zone. He lives in the friend zone."

Fisher took his shot, missed and faced his cousin. "I'd rather be in the friend zone than some one-night hookup." His interest in Kylee extended beyond the bedroom. Not that he hadn't thought about that, but—

"Really?" Toben asked, tilting his hat back on his head and arching both eyebrows. "Well, hell, Fisher, that's just…wrong."

Fisher grinned, shaking his head at Toben. Since Ryder was now a happily married man, Toben had gladly taken up the reins as the town playboy. He was good-looking, sweet-talking and drew women like moths to a flame. But Fisher didn't envy Toben, he envied Ryder. Maybe he was lazy, but Fisher had never enjoyed the dating scene. He wanted to share his home with a woman who loved him, a woman he loved above all else. Their home would be full of happiness and laughter. Eventually he hoped he'd have kids—a full house that was always busy and inviting.

Brook laughed, the husky timbre drawing appreciative looks from both Jarvis and Toben. Fisher shook his head. She was pretty, her bright, curly red hair and large brown eyes signaling her vivacious personality.

And since she was new in town, she'd probably get lots of interest. Knowing her the way he was beginning to, she could handle it. She'd probably enjoy it.

"Looks like Mrs. Callahan's waving you over," Jarvis murmured.

Fisher glanced at the table of silver-haired women. "You can dance, Jarvis. So can you, Toben. Those sweet old gals can teach you a thing or two on the dance floor."

Toben snorted dismissively.

"You, Fisher Boone, are a real gentleman," Brook said, smiling up at him. "You keep holding doors open, dancing with little old ladies and being your charming self and that mystery girl will fall head over heels for you."

Fisher handed his pool cue to Brook. "I'll hold you to that." He crossed the wooden-planked floor and tipped his hat to Sylvia Callahan. "Mrs. Callahan."

"Fisher," she said, smiling sweetly. "I must say, this is one of my favorite songs."

"Well, then, let's not waste it." He offered her his hand.

Mrs. Callahan took it and let him lead her out onto the dance floor. She might be stiff with age, but she could still two-step something fierce.

"You look so much like your momma," Mrs. Callahan said. "Same eyes. Course, she was a might shorter than you."

He laughed. "Most people are."

"You musta drank a lot of milk growing up," she continued. "So big and strong. Why aren't you settled down yet, Fisher? Never thought I'd see the day when Ryder got hitched before you or your sister."

He nodded, letting her prattle on while they danced. She'd been a friend of his mother's. When his mother died, these were the ladies who had kept his family fed, cleaned the house and done the shopping until his dad got back on his feet. He couldn't see them without giving them hugs and offering them a nice word or a teasing smile as well as the occasional dance. It was the least he could do to repay their kindness. And while he knew they missed having dance partners, he suspected there was more to it. Teddy Boone was quite the catch. Every one of these ladies was sweet on his father. But if they were hoping he'd give them some magic word to win his father they'd be disappointed. Fisher didn't have the heart to tell them that his father was, and always would be, in love with Fisher's mother.

As the music came to a close, he spun Mrs. Callahan. She was giggling and breathless when he escorted her back to her table.

"My turn." Brook stood at his elbow. "If you're free?"

He nodded. "Think you can keep up?" he asked, nodding at the stage. The beat was quick, and two other couples were spinning like tops across the wooden floor.

"I've been watching YouTube videos for this." Brook watched them, wide-eyed. "Try me."

By the time the music was over, Fisher was limping.

"I'm so sorry," Brook said, laughing. "It's harder than it looks."

"Are you wearing steel-toed boots?" he asked.

She burst out laughing again.

"It's his fault, not yours," Toben interrupted. "He never could lead worth a damn." He held his hand out to Brook.

Fisher looked back and forth between them, inwardly groaning. Brook had wanted to see some of Stonewall Crossing and meet the locals. Toben would definitely give her a warm welcome.

"You're telling me you can do better?" Brook asked, inspecting his cousin.

"Why don't you see for yourself, darlin'?" Toben tipped his hat back.

Fisher shook his head. "I'm getting a beer." He headed toward the bar—to find Kylee staring at him. Her blue eyes looked huge in her pale face and her black hair fell over one shoulder down to her waist...a waist that was visible since she was wearing clothes that actually fitted her.

And, damn, the curves of her body made him ache. She looked so pretty his chest hurt, pressing in on him until he felt light-headed. She might make his body stand up and take notice, but it was more than physical attraction. When she smiled, he smiled. When she laughed, he wanted to hear her do it again. He wanted to sit beside her, to see her and take care of her.

She had a smile on her face when he sat on a bar stool—a smile that made it hard to say, "Hi," without sounding like an idiot.

"Doc." She nodded as Devon slid a tub of clean beer tumblers and glasses in front of her. "Beer?" Kylie asked, barely glancing at him.

"Yes, please." He accepted the bottle she slid his way. "Looks like a quiet night."

She nodded, wiping out a tumbler before putting it away. Her gaze swept the room, one of her habits he was beginning to recognize.

"How was your week?" he asked.

"Fine." But she didn't look at him. She started unloading the tub, sliding glasses into the overhead slots and stacking the tumblers on the shelf behind her.

"Mine was long, thanks for asking. Got myself a

dog—he's a real handful. Some crazy woman saved him from being eaten by two big dogs." He watched her reaction. She had the sweetest smile he'd ever seen. "Chance has more energy than three dogs combined. Archer's not exactly thrilled but…" He shrugged. "And I spent a couple of nights working at Archer's place—"

"To get your house back?" she asked, glancing at him.

He nodded. "I like to think I'm helping my brother gain his independence." He grinned. "*And* I have a new surgical resident. Which means training." He nodded his head at the dance floor where Brook and Toben were spinning like crazy. "If there was a surgery or an emergency this week, I think we worked it."

"She's a veterinarian?" Kylee asked, looking at the couple.

He nodded. "Really good, too, as far as I can tell. She's smart and gets along with everyone—even Archer, so far. That says a lot. Part of my job is to show her the ropes." Was it his imagination or did Kylee's mouth tighten? "Though it looks like Toben wants to take over."

Kylee glanced at him then. "You sure that's a good idea?"

He laughed. "She's a big girl. What she does with her free time is her business."

Kylee's gaze met his.

"You're up," Devon called, holding a large tray of pints high.

"Got it." Kylee's gaze left his as she headed down the bar to a waiting customer.

He watched her move, the way her new jeans hugged her hips and thighs when she bent and stretched. Her long hair swayed with every step, slipping over her shoulder to shield her face. He wanted to tuck it back, to run his fingers through its silky strands. He clenched his fists, hoping to redirect his focus. But then she bent forward, her shirt clinging to her chest and driving him to the edge. His grip on his beer bottle grew dangerously tight as he took a long swig.

"That's her?" Brook asked, coming to sit beside him at the bar. "She's gorgeous."

He nodded, never taking his eyes off Kylee. Hell, he could stare at her all night.

"Toben's right. You're whipped, Dr. Boone," Brook's words were soft, but he heard her amusement.

Fisher shot Brook a look. "Thanks for the opinion."

"What can I get you?" Kylee asked, drawing his attention back to her—and those blue eyes. His throat felt tight.

"I'll have what he's having," Brook said.

He shot Brook a look. "Kylee, this is Brook Marcus, the new surgical resident at the hospital."

"All the way from New York," Brook agreed. "Nice to meet you."

Kylee nodded, the slightest smile on her face. "You, too." She popped the top off a beer bottle before setting it on the bar.

The song on the jukebox changed and Brook hopped up. "I can dance to this without breaking your toes, cowboy."

He glanced at Kylee. She drew in a deep breath, her big blue eyes shifting from him to Brook. He'd give just about anything to know what she was thinking.

"Come on," Brook continued, pulling him from the bar.

He left his beer on the counter and let her lead him onto the dance floor.

Brook chuckled, moving to the beat. "I think you should ask her out, Fisher."

"If only it were that easy," he muttered.

She stared up at him. "Nobody said it was easy to get what you want."

He laughed then. She was right. And, no matter what Kylee had been through, he wanted a chance to prove things could be better. Things could be good. He wanted them to be good, for her and Shawn both. He glanced at the end of the bar. Shawn sat there, pencil between his lips, staring at his notebook.

"What's holding you back?" Brook asked.

"She's been through a lot," he murmured.

"Haven't we all?"

"No, not like her." His defense was quick. "I don't want to mess things up. Or scare her off." Something about Kylee made him hesitate. She was strong, that much was clear. But she was also fragile.

Brook didn't say anything else about Kylee. Instead, she asked him about Stonewall Crossing and what the locals did for fun.

"You're doing it," he told her, laughing again. "Rodeo most weekends. Dance halls, bowling and the occasional holiday events are about it."

Brook shook her head. "This is *such* a small town."

One of the things Brook had mentioned—at least a dozen times—was how cute Stonewall Crossing was. She couldn't get over the fact that the town was smaller than her undergraduate university.

"It is," he agreed.

She looked up at him. "From the distinct pride in your voice, I'm assuming you've no grand plans to go on to bigger and better things?"

He smiled, shaking his head. "There might be bigger, but I doubt there's better." There was only one thing that could make Stonewall Crossing any better than it was. His gaze found Kylee at the bar—staring right back at him. Now he needed to get up the nerve to tell her as much.

Chapter Six

Kylee tore her gaze from Fisher. She should be happy
for him. She should want him to be happy. He deserved
it. Brook Marcus was his sort of woman. Smart, attractive, confident—an animal lover. And Brook made Fisher
laugh. He had a great laugh. Every time Kylee heard it,
she found herself grinning in response.

She should be happy for him…but watching them on
the dance floor left Kylee feeling hollow.

Since she wasn't ready to consider the reason, she
busied herself with wiping the bar down and checking
in with Shawn. He sat at the end of the bar, lost in his
work, his fingers and his forehead smudged with pencil
lead. She grinned, wiping the marks from his face. But
Shawn's drawing made her pause. Her little brother's tal-
ent was awe-inspiring. "Amazing," she whispered, giving him a quick hug. "Need anything? Hungry? Want
something to drink?"

He shook his head, barely glancing up before returning to his work, his fingers blurring the thicker lines to
give the illusion of movement.

By the time she'd restocked the towels, Brook and
Fisher were sitting at the bar. They were smiling at each
other, in deep conversation. Kylee ignored the ache that

settled in the pit of her stomach, reminding herself over and over that Fisher Boone was a friend, a good friend. And that was all he would ever be.

If she was bothered by the budding romance between Brook and Fisher, it had nothing to do with the good doctor and everything to do with being lonely. It was a choice, she knew that. But watching over Shawn, keeping them safe, hadn't left a lot of room for much else. Most of the time she managed to keep her emotions bottled up, but when she stopped long enough it was hard to ignore just how lonely she was. She wouldn't wish it on anyone. Especially someone like Fisher.

Brook spoke quickly, her hands moving and her face animated, catching Kylee's eye. With her crazy curly red hair, big brown eyes and thick dark lashes there was no denying she was pretty. What's more, she had a friendly and open sort of energy. She and Fisher could be good together.

Kylee left them alone, finding Devon to review the week's order and work schedule. She might have Saturday off, but she was working the late shift every night this week. It wasn't the hours she objected to, it was dragging Shawn along with her. Like her, he was making strides with their new life, but he still didn't like to be alone. She worried about him, his odd sleep schedule and the eclectic company he kept. But all those things came hand in hand with her working in a bar.

She waved at Devon as the other woman clocked out, then she picked up one of the large tubs for cleanup. Kylee made a sweep of the dance hall, clearing three tables and pocketing tip money before making her way back to the bar. It might be a slow night, but the table of older ladies had been generous tippers. A rare treat.

She tucked the tip into her pocket, catching sight of Shawn, yawning, at the end of the bar. If she worked at the animal hospital she wouldn't need to worry about tips or regular late-night shifts. The only thing stopping her from turning in the completed application was fear. Something she was working hard to let go of. She was smart—she could learn the skills necessary for this job. She'd strive to become the best damn employee there. And give Shawn the future he deserved.

Just like that, she made up her mind. She'd turn in the application Monday morning and do her best to be as polite as possible. If they hired her, she'd have to work on her customer-service skills—admittedly not her strong suit.

"Can we get some water?" Brook called, smiling at her.

Kylee headed back to the bar, a spring in her step. She filled two mugs with ice and water and put them on the counter. Since it was so slow, she was going to work in the supply closet. That way Fisher and Brook would have some privacy, and she'd have some space.

"Thanks. You haven't been in Stonewall Crossing all that long have you, Kylee?" Brook asked before she could disappear. "This place is a trip. I half expected to see a horse tied up out front."

"It happens now and then," Kylee agreed, thinking about Fisher's horse tied in front of Pop's bakery. She and Shawn had laughed, in total shock. From the corner of her eye, she saw Fisher glance Shawn's way. He was smiling.

"Really? I'll have to take pictures of that." Brook's brown eyes went round. "How long did it take before it started feeling normal for you?"

Kylee had to smile at that. She'd never had a normal

so she couldn't really answer the question. Instead she said, "Everyone made us feel welcome right away." Everyone, like Fisher. She glanced at him—he was looking at his beer bottle.

Her chest ached.

"So you feel at home here?" Brook pushed.

Kylee nodded, without thought. She didn't know when this small town had become home, but it was. The anxiety that gripped her had all but disappeared. She wasn't suspicious of everyone she met. There was security here—even if she and her brother were living in a tiny apartment in the back of a bar. For the first time in years, she and Shawn were safe.

"I'm not sure I could ever feel at home here," Brook laughed. "But I guess I can enjoy good beer, some pool and cowboys." She winked at Kylee.

Kylee glanced at Fisher, then back at Brook. If Fisher was interested in Brook, he needed to step up his game.

"I'm off to play some pool." Brook tipped her beer bottle at Fisher. "With some cowboys."

Kylee expected Fisher to go with her, so his, "Have fun," was a surprise. Shouldn't he be running interference between Toben and Brook instead of smiling at her from his bar stool? Sort of like how she should be heading into the supply room to double-check inventory but wasn't.

She had missed his easygoing smile and conversation. She'd missed him, being here, being him. She was beginning to think she was the only woman to appreciate just what a good man Fisher was. If Brook Marcus had any brains, she'd forget fooling around with sweet-talkers like Toben and go for the real thing—Fisher. She knew if things were different, Fisher Boone was the sort of man she'd want at her side.

"You look pretty, Kylee," Fisher said quietly. But his words made something warm and light bubble up inside her. Her heart thumped so hard and fast she worried he might hear it. But he rested an elbow on the bar. "Shawn drawing more horses? Too bad y'all didn't get here a few weeks earlier for the Fourth of July. Shawn would have gotten a kick out of all the horses. We'll have another parade for Labor Day, though." He paused, sipping his beer. "Got any special plans coming up?

She shrugged, the pounding of her heart barely slowing.

"Any interest in bowling?" he asked.

Kylee looked at him then, her eyes meeting his—and holding.

His gaze was warm and welcoming, the smile on his face too distracting to ignore. She couldn't hold back her answering smile or stop the rush of pleasure through her blood. It was easy to smile with him, to be herself. She swallowed, tearing her gaze from his.

Herself.

Broken. Vulnerable. Bitter. Confused. Fisher wouldn't want to know that girl. A girl who'd done things he could never understand. She'd never ask him to. No matter how he might make her feel, she needed to remember who she was and where she came from. They lived in different worlds and always would.

"Renata's got big things planned for Labor Day this year. The parade, a craft market, some gunfight reenactments or something—the crowds love that. I'm helping out with some hayrides, too. Maybe Shawn could help with that?" he asked, his question drawing her attention back to him. His eyes flashed and the corner of his mouth quirked in a half smile.

Her lungs felt empty. "You c-can ask him."

He nodded. "Just wanted to make sure it was okay with you first—this time."

Meaning he didn't want to upset her again. It meant a lot that he'd remembered. But Fisher would remember. Fisher would look for ways to include Shawn, too. Because that was who he was, thoughtful, caring, handsome...and off-limits. "I appreciate that, Doc." Her voice wavered.

"It's a good month away but you should plan on going." His gaze got tangled up in hers just long enough to make her dazed and speechless.

"Maybe." She glanced beyond him at Brook. "We'll keep an eye out for you two."

"Two?" he asked, a crease forming on his forehead.

She nodded. "Brook. She's new in town. You two have a lot in common."

He blinked, confusion lining his face. *"Work?"*

"She's pretty, Doc," Kylee encouraged. Was he denying what she'd seen on the dance floor? There was a spark there, a connection. "You should ask her out."

He stared at Kylee then, completely frozen.

Why was he acting so...strange? Was he uncomfortable talking about his feelings? She could relate to that. She tried again, "I know you're not a ladies' man—"

"Whoa, whoa." That snapped him out of it. "Why do you say that?"

"I've never seen you hit on anyone...or interested before." Kylee couldn't help laughing at the affront on his face.

"Before?" he asked, confusion lining his features.

"I saw you two out there." She paused, that empty, hollow ache threatening to consume her. She hurried on,

"You're into the teasing and funny thing. It makes *you* safe." He made her feel safe. Which was why, after everything she'd been through, Fisher was such a complete surprise. He was the best man she'd ever met.

He stared at her for a long time before asking, "Safe is bad?"

"No," she assured him, holding up her hands. "All I meant was… I just thought…" If he didn't get a move on, men like Toben would turn Brook's head and he'd never stand a chance. Why women were drawn to that, the Tobens of this world, she'd never understand. She glanced at the redhead, then back at Fisher. "Maybe, I could help you?"

He arched a brow. "*Help* me?"

"Get the girl," she murmured. This was for him. To see him laughing and dancing would make her happy. She wanted that for him.

The longer he sat there, his green eyes searching hers, the more uncomfortable she became. Had she offended him? She hadn't meant to. Maybe her delivery needed work. Further proof that she had no business trying to have any sort of relationship—friendship or otherwise.

"You're helping me because…?" he asked, eyes narrowed.

Her heart was in her throat. "You've been really good to Shawn and me, Doc. I appreciate it."

"I'm glad. But you don't need to pay me back, Kylee."

His words cut through her. He'd saved Chance and taken an interest in Shawn. No matter how much he denied it, she knew he had something to do with Shawn's scholarship to camp. He'd done all those things with no ulterior motive—and it humbled her. In her old world, actions or favors had costs. Jesse taught her that. This was a very different world, one she was becoming fond of, but old habits die hard.

Her experience with men was limited to Jesse. Jesse, who told her who to be nice to and taught her that if she smiled or talked to anyone else there would be painful consequences. Other than Shawn, she'd never thought of willingly being attached to a man. And feeling affection—feeling anything except fear—had never occurred to her. But nothing had prepared her for the way she felt around Fisher. He was the first man she'd liked having around, and she wanted to do something for him. Not as payback, but in appreciation. She just didn't know how to say that to him.

Something on her face must have told him she was struggling because his hand slid across the bar, reaching for hers before she realized what he was doing. The spark between his hand and hers made her whole body tremble. Whatever hollowness she felt was replaced by an altogether different feeling. Heavy, warm, aching and oh, so good. She didn't pull away, she couldn't. Instead, she stared at their hands, at his sun-bronzed fingers twined with hers. His fingertips were rough, his nails short and clean, his strength wrapped securely around her. Her heart thundered like crazy, making her shirt tremble in time with each rapid beat.

Their gazes met, turning the spark into something bigger. Something she wasn't ready to face.

She pulled her hand from his, the brush of skin on skin forcing a shiver down her spine. Whatever reaction she was having, he seemed immune. He sat there, stiffly, the muscle in his jaw locked. He seemed…angry?

Her words rushed together, "You're a good guy." Her voice was husky, her throat and lungs tight. "I haven't known many of those, but it seems fair that a good guy should get the girl." *A girl that's not me.* She nodded at the door leading into the bar. "I know Toben is related to you, but I'm pretty sure you're the better man here."

His smile was back, his posture easing as he asked, "What does helping me mean, exactly?"

"Working on your technique?" She shrugged.

He snorted. "There's nothing wrong with my technique," he argued.

"Maybe, maybe not. I haven't seen any." She laughed as he scowled at her. "We'll see—when you're ready."

"Oh, I'm ready." His answer was quick. "My technique is just fine."

"Fisher," Toben called out. "We need another player. You game?"

"In a sec," he answered, glancing at the end of the bar. "I'll ask Shawn about helping me out with the parade—"

Kylee's gaze followed his. Shawn was asleep, his face pillowed on his arms. It was almost one and they'd had a long day. No wonder he was wiped out. Once he was asleep, waking him up wasn't easy.

"I'm thinking he's too big for you to carry to bed," Fisher said.

"I can do it," she insisted. But he *was* too big for her to carry. And then there was the matter of the twenty paying customers who were still her responsibility.

"I don't mind, Kylee," Fisher asserted.

She shook her head, rubbing Shawn's back to wake him up. When Shawn didn't move, she admitted defeat. She looked at Fisher, saw his smile and smiled in return. "That would be nice, Fisher, thank you." She pulled her key out of her pocket and handed it over. "Shawn, Fisher's gonna take you home, okay?" She and Fisher exchanged another smile at Shawn's muffled grunt. When Fisher scooped her little brother up, Shawn barely stirred. "Can you get the door and hold him?"

"Think so." Fisher acted like Shawn weighed nothing. And her little brother looked so small cradled against the wall of Fisher's chest. Fisher smiled down at Shawn, nodding at the sketchbook on the bar. "He's gonna want that."

He would. He'd panic if he woke up without it. Fisher knew how important Shawn's drawings were to him. More than that, Fisher regarded Shawn with genuine affection. The kind of affection her little brother wanted and deserved.

She stared up at Fisher. She knew he was strong. His chest was broad and his thickly muscled arms cradled Shawn. But his strength came from the inside. He was every bit a real man—while remaining kind and gentle. A kind and gentle man who made her ache deep down inside.

"Kylee?" he asked, his voice low.

She needed to stop looking at him, stop feeling these feelings…

"Can I get a drink down here?" a customer called to her.

"I got him." Fisher carried Shawn through the Employees Only door.

She filled a pitcher for the customer and cleared off the bar, her mind racing. It was important that she understood the difference between friendship and a romantic relationship. Just because Fisher was being nice to her didn't mean he was looking for more from her. If she was overreacting to him, supersensitive to him, it was because she'd never been in this situation before. She'd never had a male friend, she'd never wanted one before.

But, try as she might, she couldn't dismiss that she was grappling with something more than friendship.

"He's out." Fisher reappeared. "Barely moved when I put him on the bed."

"Thanks." She nodded, working hard to keep herself calm and collected. "I appreciate it."

"Looks nice in there." He smiled. "You painted?"

She nodded. She'd left the windows cracked to air out the fumes. She could only hope the window screens were in decent enough shape to keep creepy crawlers outside where they belonged.

"Not too cramped?" He was looking at her again, in that intense way. "Sharing a bed with your brother can't be fun."

"Oh, no, I sleep in the recliner. He's a karate expert— in his sleep." She smiled, admitting, "It might seem cramped but we're pretty happy. My little brother has a roof over his head, food in his stomach and an actual bed to sleep in. I couldn't ask for much more."

Fisher's jaw locked again. He opened his mouth, then closed it and swallowed. She waited, knowing he had something to say. But not sure she wanted to hear it.

"Fisher," Toben called out. "You coming or not?"

"You should go." She glanced at Brook. "Maybe try flirting?"

He cocked an eyebrow. "I don't know if I'm up for it. What with my lack of technique and all."

She bit back a grin. "Have a nice night, Fisher. And thanks again." She picked up a bottle of cleaner and a new rag, and started wiping down the empty tables. He must have stood there, watching her, for a few more minutes because Toben yelled again before Fisher joined them at the pool table.

It was only later, when she was lying on the recliner, that she realized she might have made a mistake. Jesse had taught her how to flirt, how to *get* a man, but what she'd been after wasn't their hearts. Jesse was very territorial. He'd never said he loved her, but she was definitely his. When Jesse wanted sex, it had always been awkward and quick. In all their time together, he'd never offered her sweet words, soft kisses, or taken the time to explore her body. They'd never had the opportunity to be naked—not with Shawn around. She had *no* business criticizing the way Fisher pursued a woman or who he should have a relationship with. She had no experience with anything real.

There was only one thing Kylee was 100 percent certain of. If Brook didn't see how lucky she was—how great Fisher was—she didn't deserve him.

"A RECLINER?" RENATA ASKED, laying a napkin at each place setting at the large dining table.

Fisher nodded. He'd given up pretending to his sister that he wasn't interested in Kylee. Maybe it was the twin thing, but she always saw right through him anyway. What he needed was a sounding board. And Renata was a girl—she might be able to shed a little light on Kylee's offer to help him win Brook, too.

He'd shared what limited information he had with Renata, desperate for some sort of insight. But his sister's theory on Kylee and Shawn's past had turned his blood cold—before igniting it with white-hot anger.

"If she's spent her whole life protecting Shawn and surviving, she's probably never had a relationship." Renata glanced at him.

"Shawn mentioned someone named Jesse." Fisher

looked at his sister. "All he said was the name and they both locked up in fear."

Renata sighed, shaking her head. "Poor things."

"Don't let her hear you say that." Fisher grinned, admiring Kylee's independence. "I don't know what I was expecting. I guess I was hoping for something better than a tiny, grungy apartment. At the back of a bar, for crying out loud." He shook his head. "They have practically nothing. A couch, a recliner and a chest of drawers. No table, no chairs, no curtains, no television." The bright off-yellow paint job had only made the stark sadness of the place that much more obvious. "She wasn't pulling my leg, either. She's…content with the way things are." When Kylee didn't have her guard up, her face revealed a lot.

"That bothers you?" Renata asked, nudging him so he'd focus on his work.

He set a knife and fork on a napkin. "No." He paused, straightening the utensils. "Yes. Of course it does. What the hell have they been through to think that place is okay?" He shook his head. "Remember dad's old workshop? Before we built the Lodge?"

Renata wrinkled her nose. "Yes."

"The place isn't much better than that."

Maybe he was too accustomed to the good life. He wasn't wasteful or self-indulgent, his parents had made sure of that. It didn't matter that the Boones owned all the land in and around Stonewall Crossing, his father raised them to work hard and count every dollar they earned. Hell, he'd worked extra hours and odd jobs for several years, pinching pennies and living in one of the old bunkhouses so he could build the house he wanted. And he had. While he'd never thought his twenty-two-hundred-square-foot house was overly large, seeing the space Shawn and Kylee were calling home made him rethink things.

"What's really bothering you, little brother?" Renata asked. "It's pretty obvious you like her, so why not—"

"She offered to help me," he said, shaking his head. "She offered to help my with my technique…so I could get Brook Marcus."

"Brook Marcus?" Renata asked. "The new resident? Do you want Brook Marcus?"

"No," Fisher answered. "I want Kylee."

Renata grinned.

Fisher groaned, rolling his eyes. "Come on, now."

"No, no, give me a minute." Renata sighed. "You are in love for the first time. I have a right to savor it."

"Savor it later," he muttered. "What do I do about this Brook thing?"

"I think you should take Kylee up on her offer," she answered immediately. His sister went back to laying out the napkins, smoothing the tablecloth into place before she asked, "Why not? You'll get to spend time with Kylee, right?"

"I guess but—"

"No buts." Renata frowned at him. "Time is a good thing. From the little time I've spent with her, she's as skittish as one of Archer's rescue horses. Jumpy, wary and full of fear." She looked at Fisher. "She's going to have scars, Fisher. I'm thinking they might be pretty deep, too. You know that, right?"

He nodded. He'd thought a lot about that. "We all do. Just some are deeper than others."

Renata sat the napkins on the table and hugged him. "I

wish you'd let that go, Fisher. It was an accident. You're a big guy—"

"A big guy who almost killed his best friend." Fisher shook his head. Vince wasn't that much smaller than him, but remembering his friend unconscious on the mat—then hooked up to tubes in the hospital—still made him sick to his stomach.

"You were boxing," Renata reminded him.

Fisher kissed his sister's cheek and stepped away from her. "I know, I was there. It was my last fight." It had been years, but sometimes it felt like yesterday. He went back to setting the table. "All I'm saying is I won't hold her past against her. She's been through a lot, but she's still standing. I respect that." If she'd give him a chance, he'd make sure she and Shawn were taken care of.

Renata blew out a deep breath. "You're a good man, Fisher Boone."

"I sure am," he replied, teasing.

Fifteen minutes later the house was filling up. Meaning all of his brothers and their families were here. Hunter, his wife, Josie, and their son, Eli. Ryder, his very pregnant wife, Annabeth, and their son, Cody. Then there was Archer, their father, Teddy, Annabeth's grandmother Florence, and cousin Tandy.

Plus Cutter, Shawn and Kylee. Seeing her here made his chest swell with pride. His brothers might argue with him, but he knew she was the prettiest girl here. Even if she did look lost and uncomfortable. Once the initial greetings were over, Fisher watched Eli pull Shawn and Cody aside, the three smiling and laughing in no time.

When everyone found a seat, Kylee sat stiffly on a large ottoman. Fisher sat beside her, wishing there was something he could do to ease her anxiety.

Teddy was all smiles for Kylee. "I hear you've moved from Las Vegas. The city that never sleeps to the city that shuts down tight at nine o'clock. Must be quite a change." He paused. "Guess you can't really consider Stonewall Crossing much of a city, either."

Kylee smiled, her nerves obvious. "I don't think so, sir. But I—we—like it here."

"She's taking to it like a fish takes to water," Cutter added.

"Good. It's a real nice place to raise a family." Teddy went on, "A young man like Shawn will find lots to do that will keep him out of trouble."

Fisher saw the love on her face when she looked at her brother. "I'm counting on it."

"Renata says he's going to camp next week?" Hunter asked. "Eli will be there, too. He looks forward to it all year."

Kylee nodded. "He can't wait."

"Fisher told me Shawn's quite the artist," Josie spoke up.

"Always drawin'," Cutter agreed.

"He is." Kylee glanced at the old man with true affection. "He reads a lot of comic books and graphic novels. I think he's good enough to illustrate one."

"I'd really love to see his work," Josie said.

"Josie writes and illustrates children's books." Fisher pointed at the large painting over the huge stone fireplace on the back wall. "That's hers."

Kylee stared at the painting, her eyes going round.

"Where are my manners?" Renata jumped up. "What can I get you to drink? Cutter? Flo? Kylee?"

"A beer sounds good to me." Ryder said.

"Ryder," Annabeth spoke up, laughing. "Your sister

does not need to wait on you. You know your way around the kitchen just fine."

"I had to try, princess." Ryder kissed her cheek. "You want anything?"

"Um, to deliver these babies?" Annabeth said, making everyone laugh.

"I hope the sonogram is wrong and they're both girls," Renata said. "Though I'm not sure your husband could handle being the father to two girls. They'd never date."

"One girl is more than enough." Ryder dragged a hand over his face. "And I'm sure as hell not ready to talk about my daughter dating already."

Fisher laughed, knowing Renata was right. After spending years as the ultimate heartbreaker, Ryder was going to have an extrahard time when his little girl, or girls, grew up.

"How much longer?" Kylee asked softly.

"Six weeks." Ryder and Annabeth spoke in unison, making everyone laugh again.

"You quit trying to rush those babies," Flo jumped in. "Once they get here, there's no going back."

"I know." Annabeth took her grandmother's hand in hers. "You're right. I just miss sitting comfortably. And not getting up to go to the restroom ten times a night. And not having indigestion. And the sight of my feet."

"You make pregnancy sound so tempting," Josie said.

As the pregnancy talk continued, Fisher glanced at Kylee from the corner of his eye. She was staring around the room, getting her bearings. While Shawn seemed at ease, Kylee wasn't. She had that jumpiness he hadn't seen in a while.

He leaned closer to murmur, "Can I show you around? There's a great view outside."

She blinked, looking at him. "I don't want to be rude."

"You're not. This is the only night the Lodge wasn't booked up with guests, so dad wanted to get the family together," Fisher explained.

"So, it's like a hotel?" she asked, seeming relieved. "Oh."

He smiled. "Dad hates being on his own."

She nodded. "Your mom?" Her blue eyes met his. "It's none of my business—"

"She died when I was in high school." Fisher explained. "He still misses her."

"That never goes away."

"Miss her every damn day," Fisher agreed.

"Mine, too," Kylee's words were soft. "My mom, I mean."

Her words opened the door to a dozen questions. What had happened to her mother? How long had she been alone? Who had hurt her and Shawn? And how had they ended up in Stonewall Crossing? "So, a quick tour?"

Her attention wandered back to the rest of his family, laughing and talking among themselves. The boys had relocated to a table in the corner, two stacks of playing cards and several game boxes piled on the edge. "Okay," she agreed.

He took her outside first, where the view from the deck was amazing. The sun was descending, turning the sky shades of purple and deep blue edged in a fiery red. Even with the sun on its way to bed, there was no denying the heat. The breeze was soft, but didn't do much to ease the temperature.

"It's beautiful." She spoke with such yearning that he turned her way.

She was staring, openmouthed, at the scene before her.

From their vantage point, she could see the rolling hills speckled with livestock, shadowed valleys and the distant creek. The ranch was his home; he knew it like the back of his hand. But there were times the beauty of the land left even him speechless. Watching her, he wondered if he'd ever seen something as beautiful.

"Been in my family for generations," he murmured, getting lost in the swell of her lips, the curve of her cheek and the sweep of her long dark lashes.

"Generations…" She breathed the word. "You grew up here?"

"Pretty much."

"And now?" she asked, turning to face him.

"Dad divided up the property between us. I have a house," he said, pointing behind her. "On that hill, the far side. Being there, it's almost like I'm the only one out here."

"You like that?" she asked, her blue eyes searching his. "To be alone?"

"Sometimes. I have a big family." He looked at the door with meaning. "Sometimes I need the quiet, the space, to be me."

She nodded, a slight smile on her face.

"Which is a lot easier when Archer isn't living with me," he added with a chuckle.

"Oh." She paused. "Yes, he's…"

"Prickly? Antisocial? A curmudgeon?" Fisher loved seeing her laugh. "Lacking social graces? Crusty? Opinionated?"

She held up her hand, still laughing. "He has a strong personality."

He nodded, thinking over her description. "I think you

nailed that on the head. You could also replace *strong* with *difficult*."

She shook her head, still smiling. "Why is he staying with you?"

"Water pipe broke. He lives in one of the original ranch buildings, over a hundred years old. I'm not sure why, since it's barely standing and it's nothing special to look at. It'd probably be easier to knock it down and start over, but that would take time. And, as you might have picked up on, Archer isn't a patient sort." He shrugged. "So, until the place is fixed, I invited him to stay with me. Now I get to enjoy the pleasure of his company every single day."

She nodded. "Sounds about right."

He cocked a brow. "Meaning?"

"You…you would do something like that." She cleared her throat. "Be generous, I mean."

"First nice, now generous." His attention shifted to the barn and lookout tower. "Is that another strike against me?"

"There are no strikes against you, Fisher." Her voice was low, but he heard her.

In the fading sunlight, her eyes were crystal blue. Her cheeks were pink, but he hoped it had nothing to do with the lingering heat of the day. He wanted to be the reason she blushed and her breath hitched. More than anything, he wanted to be the reason for her blinding smiles.

"I like the sound of that," he murmured, fighting the urge to take her hand in his. He ached to touch her.

"We just need to figure out how to show Dr. Marcus what a catch you are." Kylee smiled, turning her attention back to the ranch.

Disappointment hit him hard, right in the gut.

"Kylee?" Shawn stepped out onto the back deck, followed by Eli. "Didn't know where you were."

Fisher watched the exchange—Kylee's apology, Shawn's anxiety. His sister's warning filled his ears. *She's going to have scars, Fisher. I'm thinking they might be pretty deep.* It wasn't only Kylee's past he'd have to deal with. Shawn and Eli were about the same age, but inside he suspected Shawn's life experiences had aged him. Eli radiated confidence and humor. Shawn was uncertain and wary.

"I wanted her to see the view before it was too dark," Fisher explained, waving Shawn closer. "See that building down there?" he asked. "That's the horse barn."

Shawn pushed the hair from his eyes and leaned against the railing. "The big white one?"

"That's the one. Thought maybe after we eat I could take you down there. Camp starts next week, so this would be like a preview," Fisher offered.

"You can meet Red," Eli offered. "He's my horse."

Shawn glanced at Kylee. "Can we?"

"Definitely," Kylee agreed, hesitating briefly before asking, "Fisher, you said something about needing help with the hayrides?"

His insides shifted. She was giving him her trust. He liked it. "I'm leading the hayrides in a few weeks, for Labor Day. I need someone to help out. Check harnesses, give the horses water and replace hay bales as we go. Eli said he'd help, so I need one more set of hands."

Shawn looked between the two of them. "Really? I mean, I don't know anything about harnesses or hay bales—"

"I'll teach you," Fisher interrupted.

"Me, too," Eli offered.

Fisher grinned at his nephew. "You'll be a pro in no time."

Shawn's smile gutted him. The boy didn't smile enough. He didn't complain or pout, he just never seemed happy. "I'll do my best, Doc."

"I know you will," Fisher agreed.

"Hey, there you are." Renata poked her head out. "Dinner's ready. Hope you have some room in your refrigerators. You'll be taking some leftovers home with you. Dad went a little crazy in the kitchen. If you don't take some home, we'll be eating beans, brisket and coleslaw for a month."

Shawn and Eli hurried back inside while Kylee lingered at the railing. "It's just so pretty," she said. "I've never seen anything like it."

"Take your time, Kylee, there's no rush." He left her staring out at the hills, content that she was there—a part of his world.

Chapter Seven

Fisher didn't say much on the ride from the Lodge to the horse barn. Eli was doing a fine job of keeping the conversation going. Shawn's occasional grunt or one- or two-word answers was all Eli needed to keep talking. Archer sat beside him in the front, lost in his own thoughts.

"We have between fifteen and twenty horses here," Eli was saying.

"More, if you count the rehabilitation center," Archer added.

Fisher smiled at the pride in his brother's voice. Archer might be a "strong personality," but his heart was in the right place—especially when it came to horses. He loved horses more than anything in the world. That included most people.

"Why do horses need rehab?" Shawn asked. "I thought that was drinking and drugs and stuff."

"Luckily, most animals don't need that sort of rehab," Fisher said. "Archer takes in animals that have been neglected, abandoned or abused. He helps them heal, body and spirit. And, when they're ready, he helps them find a home." He finished, aware that Archer was watching him. "What?"

"Nothing," Archer murmured, a smile on his face.

Fisher parked, barely out of the truck before Eli and Shawn ran into the barn.

"Think they're excited?" Fisher asked, reaching to the dashboard to grab the bag of apples he'd brought.

"They're boys." Archer said, as if that explained everything. "Think I'll take the ATV and head out. I have some charts to review."

Fisher suspected his brother was done being sociable and knew no one here would stop him from leaving. "I'll be along later," Fisher said.

Archer paused. "You like this girl, don't you?"

Fisher regarded his brother over the hood of his truck. "Yep."

Archer nodded. Fisher waited for more of a response, but Archer said, "This weekend we should work on the foreman's house." Clearly, he wasn't spending too much time worrying over his little brother's love life. But it made Fisher smile nonetheless.

"Maybe. But Renata wanted to meet and talk about Labor Day prep work," Fisher reminded him.

Archer raised an eyebrow. "That's more than a month away. There's plenty of time to fix the water main and do what Renata needs, too." He paused. "If we all work together, it could happen." He headed to the shed where the all-terrain vehicles were kept.

Fisher shook his head. He was more than ready for Archer to be back in his own place, but he had a hard time believing Ryder, Hunter and Renata would see things Archer's way. Most of them were working the Labor Day events in some form or fashion because it was a big event that the Boones had always been heavily involved with. Renata had had this on the calendar for months. As ready as he was to get Archer out of his place, he suspected they would remain roommates for a while.

He headed into the barn, the faint nicker of horses and the soothing scent of hay greeting him. He'd spent countless hours here, creating some of his best memories—his first saddle, his first kiss and the first time he'd won a fight.

Eli and Shawn were already in front of Red's stall. The horse was snorting and blowing into Eli's open hand but Shawn stood back, his arms crossed, hands tucked into his armpits. Shawn might have liked the look of horses, but he wasn't ready to get up close and personal. Red was gentle, though, great with kids, or Hunter would never have allowed his son near him. But Shawn didn't know that.

"What do you think?" Eli asked.

"He's big," Shawn answered.

"Not as big as Uncle Fisher's horse." Eli stroked the side of Red's neck.

Fisher shrugged. "Have to have a big horse. I'm a big guy." He studied the boy's posture, hoping Shawn wouldn't be too intimidated. "I remember when I was little, the hardest part of riding was getting on the horse. It looked like a long way up. And once I was up, it looked like an even longer way down."

"Ever fall off?" Shawn asked.

Fisher shook his head. "When I was a boy? No. My dad only put me on sure-footed, reliable horses." He paused. "I can tell you this much, you treat a horse right, he'll be your friend for life."

Shawn regarded Red again. "Ever get stepped on?"

"Why do you think a cowboy wears boots?" Eli asked.

"We just bought me some." Shawn mumbled. "Do all the horses stay here? Where's yours, Fisher?"

"Waylon?" Fisher asked. "He's out here. You've met him before, haven't you?" He led the boys down the row of stalls and from the barn to one of the small corrals out back. Waylon must have seen the truck because the large buckskin was waiting at the fence. His ears cocked forward as he whinnied in greeting.

"Now, that's a big horse," Eli said.

"That he is," Fisher agreed. Red barely reached fourteen hands. Waylon was a quarter horse–Belgian cross, heavily muscled and sixteen-plus hands tall. But he was agile and sweet tempered, and Waylon and Fisher understood each other. Fisher had taken one look at the horse and known the two of them would be a good team. He'd been right. Waylon followed him around like a dog, content to be in Fisher's company. He and Chance hadn't hit it off yet, but Fisher had high hopes the two would become fast friends and the three of them would enjoy riding the trails together.

"Did I tell you about Chance?" he asked, handing the apples to Shawn.

"What about him?" Shawn frowned. "Is he okay? Did he get sick?"

"He's great. Got so energetic and busy I had to take him home so he didn't get in the way," Fisher said, chuckling. "I figured it'd be too crowded to bring him tonight, since he's still learning his manners."

Shawn smiled. "I bet he'll love it out here. I know I would. All this room to run is good for him, isn't it?"

"It is. He's a handful, let me tell you," Fisher said, stepping closer to Waylon. The horse head-butted him, blowing hard against his chest. "Chasing cows. He chased a raccoon up a tree, and I had to drag him inside to get him to stop barking."

"So his leg isn't bothering him?" Shawn asked, smiling.

"It's not slowing him down," Fisher promised.

"I'm glad." Shawn looked at him. "I appreciate you fixing him up, Dr. Fisher. And tonight, too. It's the first night we've gone out since we moved here. Anyway, most of the time Kylee's working."

Fisher nodded. Maybe he could get Kylee's permission to bring Shawn riding a few nights this week. It would be better if the boy wasn't so uneasy on the first day of camp. "Bet he smells the apples." Eli laughed as Waylon gave him a gentle nudge.

Fisher scratched Waylon's forelock and patted his neck reassuringly. "You think so?" He glanced at the boys.

Shawn grinned as the horse nudged him again. "I think he does."

"Go ahead." Fisher paused. "The trick is to keep your hand flat. Waylon doesn't want fingers, just apples."

It took a few minutes for Shawn to get up the nerve to put his hand out. Fisher stayed close by, stroking the horse's neck and talking in a low, soothing voice. He knew Waylon liked that, and maybe it would ease Shawn, too. The last thing he wanted was for Shawn to have a bad experience with a horse.

Shawn smiled from ear to ear when Waylon crunched the apple from his hand.

"There they are," Renata said, leading Josie and Kylee toward them. "Always showing off Waylon, the big *man* on the ranch."

"Look at him. He's a damn fine horse. You can't deny

it. Can they, Waylon?" Fisher asked as Waylon snuffled his neck and head.

Kylee's laugh reached him through the others. All night he'd tried not to react to her voice, her smile and the occasional laugh. He tried not to give his brothers teasing ammunition or do anything to make Cutter or his father suspect he was sweet on Kylee. At one point, Florence had announced that she wouldn't forgive him for not inviting her to their wedding.

While he'd tried not to choke on his mouthful of beans, Annabeth assured her grandmother that the invitations had yet to go out. Poor Flo's dementia came and went, making conversation somewhat challenging. But Kylee's reaction to Flo's bewildered expression had touch him deeply. She'd smiled kindly, taken Flo's hand in hers and offered to refill her drink.

Kylee hadn't said much during dinner. She was polite and helpful—clearing the table and helping out with Flo and the boys without being asked. He couldn't know for certain, but she'd seemed to enjoy herself. He hoped so. His family was big and loud, but they were good people.

Waylon rumbled low in his chest and leaned against the fence. Fisher smiled, stepping close enough for Waylon to rest his chin on the back of Fisher's shoulder. Waylon was a hugger. It tickled Fisher that something as big as Waylon could be so loving and affectionate. Fisher patted the side of Waylon's neck. When Waylon lifted his head, Fisher caught sight of Kylee's reaction. Was it his imagination or did she look like she was going to cry?

"Did you wash your hair in cologne?" Renata asked.

"He loves me," Fisher shot back, watching Kylee. But she was focused on Waylon, mystified. He'd grown up around animals, he knew how capable of affection they were. But maybe she didn't.

"You are pretty easy to love," Josie teased. "Even if you are freakishly big."

"It's all part of my charm," he countered.

"Kylee," Shawn called her closer.

Kylee was at his side, staring up at him and the horse. "What's he saying?"

"He wants a proper introduction," he said, stepping back from the horse. "Waylon, this pretty lady right here is Kylee. Kylee, this big, beautiful beast is Waylon."

Waylon nickered softly, making Kylee chuckle. "What did he say?" she asked, watching the horse.

"He said it was mighty fine to meet you." Fisher added, "And he'd be honored if you'd feed him an apple." He paused.

"All that?" she reached out, hesitant.

"Trust me, horse is my second language." He watched her, her fingers running along Waylon's neck.

"Here, Kylee." Shawn offered her an apple.

She took it, smiling when Waylon sniffed around her chest and head.

"Keep your hand flat," Shawn said. "That way your fingers don't get chomped."

Kylee glanced at Shawn, then Fisher, then Waylon. "You won't bite me, will you?" she asked quietly. She kept her hand flat as Waylon devoured the apple.

"Who will Shawn ride for camp, Uncle Fisher?" Eli asked.

"I was thinking Soldier," Fisher said, tearing his gaze from Kylee to check with his sister.

"Or Trigger," Renata added.

Fisher nodded. "Both are good, even-tempered, sure-footed horses."

"I'll show you," Eli said.

Shawn and Eli sprinted off, running in and out of the light halos cast by the lamps mounted along the fence line. Renata and Josie ambled after them.

"He's really beautiful," Kylee whispered, her fingers sliding through Waylon's mane. Waylon turned into her, head-butting her shoulder and whiffling her hair. She giggled, stroking the horse's forelock. "What is it?"

She looked beautiful, her smile so sweet he felt its warmth deep inside of him. He swallowed the lump in his throat. "He likes you."

"I doubt that," she argued, amused. "He likes apples."

Fisher regarded her closely. "It's possible he likes both."

She glanced at him. "I guess." She patted Waylon's shoulder, finally aware that they were alone. "Any progress with Brook?"

He frowned. "Define progress."

"Have you asked her out?" She paused. "Told her she's pretty?"

"Is that what I'm supposed to do?" he asked, giving Waylon a final pat before making his way back to the barn.

"If she was here right now, what would you do?" she asked, walking at his side.

He shrugged.

"What do you want to do?" she asked.

He paused, looking at her. She stopped, waiting. He knew exactly what he wanted to do—and it had nothing to do with Brook. He took her hand slowly, gently pulling her closer. Her eyes went round as he placed her hand on his chest and slid his arms around her waist. His heart was pounding like a jackhammer and his lungs were all but empty, but he didn't stop. He bent his head, cradling one soft cheek in the palm of his hand, and kissed her. It was a soft, light, slow kiss, just enough to feel the softness of her lips, the curve of her fingers as she plucked at his shirt and the rasp of their mixed breaths.

He should lift his head, put some space between them, but she was holding on to him—not pushing him away. And he wasn't ready to let go.

He ran his nose along her temple and jaw, his arms tightening the slightest bit as his mouth touched hers. He kissed one corner of her mouth, then the other, lingering on the fullness of her lower lip. She gasped, her lips parting just enough to let him in. The touch of her tongue, the heat of her breath, the feel of her body pressed tight against his…he couldn't stop the soft groan that tore from him.

He pulled back, staring down at her. She looked as dazed as he felt—if that was possible.

He could tell her, right now, what he was thinking. It might cost him her friendship. It probably *would* cost him her friendship. Deep down he knew she wasn't ready to hear what he wanted to say. He forced out, "That's what I want to do."

She blinked, her arms sliding from around his neck.

He cleared his throat, releasing her. The air between them crackled and he ached to pull her close again, to have her curves against him and her mouth beneath his. He cleared his throat again. "I think Shawn should come ride with me." Hopefully she didn't hear how gruff he sounded. "Get him more familiar with horses."

"Oh." She crossed her arms over her chest, looking lost.

"You cold?" he asked, rubbing his hands up and down her arms.

She shook her head.

"What do you think?"

"About what?" she asked, her gaze lingering on his mouth. He almost reached for her then.

"About Shawn. I can pick him up when I get off work. Bring him out to ride for a while. Only if it's okay with you. A few times, maybe." He paused, adding, "He'll enjoy camp more if he's not scared of the horses."

"Okay." She nodded but he could tell she wasn't listening. She headed into the barn before he could think of something—anything—to say. He ended up standing there, staring after her. He knew there was a connection between them, but that kiss had clinched it for him. What would Kylee do if she knew the truth? What would she do if she knew he was falling in love with her?

DONNA SHOWED HER how to use the patient data label machine. "I know it's outdated, but the school will use it until there's no way to repair it or they get some sort of money to replace it with something better." Donna grinned. "Which isn't likely to happen."

Kylee watched Donna carefully. So far, she'd almost filled a legal pad with notes. And she had the operations manual to take home and study. She could do this. It was more responsibility than she'd realized, but once she figured out what she was doing, she'd be a great patient account supervisor.

If they were going to stay in Stonewall Crossing, they couldn't keep living off the generosity of others. What would happen when she and Shawn wore out their welcome? She couldn't let that happen. If she could take care of them, no one else had to.

"When do I do this?" Kylee asked. "At the end of the day?"

Donna checked the clock. "I normally run all the cards at four. By then most owners have called to confirm or cancel so you're not wasting time or cards."

Kylee nodded. So far, everything made sense. Surgeries arrived at seven thirty. Reminder calls for the next day went out after lunch and before the afternoon patients were officially registered. Appointments ran from eight to eleven, then again from one to three. Then she would preregister patients for the next days' schedule. Admissions were a piece of cake.

Next week Donna was going to teach her the patient discharge procedures: processing payments, setting up payment plans, closing out accounts, insurance and scheduling appointments.

"You're doing great, kiddo." Donna smiled. "Take it slow and easy."

Kylee smiled back. "Thanks."

Her head was swimming with names but, thankfully, everyone wore a name badge. And scrubs. She'd never worn a uniform before, but it was nice not to have to worry about having the right clothes. The hospital gave her three pairs of maroon scrubs with white piping, deep pockets, and the University of East Texas Veterinary Teaching Hospital logo embroidered on the chest.

Donna was amazing. Knowing she wasn't fully retiring until Christmas was a huge bonus. By then, Kylee hoped she'd have absorbed every piece of information, observation or insight Donna passed on to her. One thing Donna made clear from the beginning—know who the vet techs were. According to Donna, they were the ones "in the trenches." And the ones Kylee needed to keep happy.

Part of her responsibilities was supervising two other clerks working the front desk. Glenna had handled admissions for several years and knew her stuff. When Kylee asked her why she hadn't applied for the supervisor position, Glenna had said she was hoping to go back to school and didn't want the extra responsibility.

Brad worked the discharge side, processing payments and closing out patient files. He'd been there for longer than Glenna but he, too, was a student and didn't want the hassle of a promotion. Somehow Kylee, the only one who had no previous experience, was supposed to *supervise* them. Her plan was to spend the weekend pouring over the manual so she wouldn't be quite so lost next week.

Everyone had been welcoming and professional. She knew the surgical techs already. While she wasn't thrilled that Jarvis called her *angel* and was a little too flirty with her whenever he saw her, he seemed to be that way with everyone so she let it go. Mario was more soft-spoken.

Kylee hadn't learned the clinic techs, lab techs or floating techs yet. Or the veterinarians—besides the Boones. But this was her first week. She'd dropped her application off Monday morning, been called in for an interview Tuesday morning and started working that afternoon. Even though it hadn't been a full week, she was glad it was almost the weekend. Her brain was swimming from information overload.

"We have a late appointment today," Donna said, sighing heavily. "Goliath is a mess, I'll tell you that up front. We have to book him late because he doesn't get along well with others. The dog is big and mean and hates Dr. Fisher with every bone in his body."

"Fisher?" How could anyone or anything hate Fisher Boone? No matter how hard she wanted to deny it, she couldn't. Fisher Boone was just as good and kind as he seemed.

And that kiss…

Her cheeks felt warm. That kiss had been for Brook. It was an amazing kiss. One that made her hate Brook Marcus a little bit. And envy her. Fisher certainly didn't need any pointers from her.

Between her time at the hospital and her shifts at the bar, she had had plenty of time to see Fisher in action. Even when she no longer needed confirmation that he was a good guy, she found herself searching him out. He was tireless, doing little things without thought. He wasn't seeking acknowledgment, he was just *doing*. Dancing with the widows' group. Helping a fourth year student deal with an angry pet owner when it wasn't his student or his patient. Giving his brother Ryder a pep talk on the phone when he finally got a five-minute break. Or making coffee in the waiting room because the desk was too slammed to do it. Things that made her stop and stare in wonder at the man.

Damn, that kiss…

Every single time she thought about it, she was left trembling. Who knew a kiss could do that to a person? Who could feel like they're on fire and want it more than anything? She'd done her best to act casual, like she wasn't aching on the inside. But every once in a while she'd catch him watching her and wonder at it.

"I know." Donna leaned closer. "It's a good thing Glenna left early today, she and Mrs. Schwartz don't get along. We're not supposed to speak badly of our patients, but that dog is evil."

"What did he do?" Kylee asked. "Why is he a patient?"

"He was protecting his property. And by protecting, I mean he went headfirst through a plateglass sliding door to get at the poor pool man cleaning out Goliath's pool."

Kylee stared at Donna. "Are you kidding me?"

Donna shook her head. "Luckily, the pool man got up a tree."

"Wait." Kylee followed Donna to the other end of the counter. "The dog was still moving *after* it went through a plateglass window?"

"He's a big dog. A mastiff-rottweiler mix. With a big temper." Donna pulled a large file from the rack and handed it to her. "He had dozens of stitches and they had to put pins in his back leg."

Kylee shuddered, imagining an animal that would break its leg and still be willing to attack. "So Goliath hates Dr. Fisher because—"

"He sees me as the source of his pain." Fisher took the file from Donna. "I was the one who operated on him. Every time he sees me, he gets poked or prodded. He doesn't like it. So he doesn't like me."

Kylee watched him flip through the chart, amazed by his calm. But, in the time she'd known him, she'd rarely seen Fisher rattled. And right now, wearing his white lab coat and stethoscope, his military style haircut just so and a light stubble on his angular jaw, he looked like he didn't have a care in the world. And…he looked handsome. Kylee swallowed. Why couldn't she see him without thinking about how it felt to be held in his arms, to remember the solid strength of his chest beneath her hands or his mouth on hers? She blew out a deep breath.

His green gaze caught hers. "How's it going?"

"Fine," she answered, breathless.

"She's smart as a whip," Donna added. "I might even retire early at this rate."

Kylee shook her head. "Oh, Donna—"

"Just messing with you." Donna smiled at her. "But you'll be fine long before I'm gone."

"Figured as much. Not that anyone can ever replace you, Donna." Fisher flashed that killer smile.

Kylee drew in a deep, slow breath. She needed to remember rule number one. No men—especially no Fisher Boone. She'd been hurt enough; she wasn't some stupid, naive girl anymore. Besides, he was interested in Dr. Marcus. That kiss had been for Dr. Marcus. And Dr. Marcus was interested in him, as far as she could tell. *They* were a good couple. *They* made sense. Her new habit of daydreaming about Fisher did not. People like Fisher Boone didn't end up with people like her.

"You keep your charm for someone young and single, Fisher Boone." Donna shook her head.

"Let me know when Goliath gets here, please. I'll be in the community clinic."

Kylee refused to look at him. "Yes, sir." She didn't look up until his footsteps faded.

She and Donna reviewed coding until Mrs. Schwartz arrived with Goliath. Kylee's first thought was that Mrs. Schwartz looked the right size to ride Goliath, not restrain him—not that she was an especially small woman. Kylee had never seen a dog that size. His head was the size of a serving platter, and his jaw was fully capable of doing serious damage. Try as she might, she couldn't help but worry about Fisher.

"Can you page Dr. Fisher?" Donna asked, clicking away on the keyboard.

Kylee picked up the phone and pressed the community clinic number.

"Dr. Fisher here."

"Hi." She paused, flustered. "Goliath is here."

"Hey, Kylee." He chuckled. "Fancy hearing from you like this. You have a great phone voice."

She laughed. "Your patient—"

"Do I have to?" he groaned. "I'll send two students up to get him."

"He's massive." She had no idea why she'd said that.

"So are his teeth."

Which made a lump form in her throat. "Be careful," she murmured.

There was a pause. "I will."

She hung up the phone, her heart hammering in her ears. She stared at the phone, cursing under her breath. She turned to Mrs. Schwartz. "They'll be right with you."

Kylee watched the two students take Mrs. Schwartz and Goliath to the back, trying to dismiss her anxiety. Fisher was a professional. He knew what he was doing.

For ten minutes, it was peaceful. Cutter and Shawn arrived early—probably because Shawn was so excited about tonight. Shawn was going to the Boone Ranch for riding lessons while Kylee worked her evening shift at Shots. Cutter drank coffee and Shawn knelt in front of the aquarium, watching and sketching the fish. There were two owners waiting to visit their animals in the hospital and another at Brad's window, checking out. And every one of them froze when the barking started. When the barking stopped, everyone relaxed. Then there was a shout. Followed by a hair-raising growl and a scream.

Shawn ran to the desk. "What's happening?"

"I'm sure it's fine," Kylee tried to reassure him.

Several students and two techs ran past the front desk and disappeared around the corner.

The desk phone rang. Donna answered it. "Yes?" Pause. "Yes? Of course." And she hung up. "Kylee, I have to get Mrs. Schwartz to the hospital."

"Need me to drive?" Cutter was on his feet.

"Cutter, yes," Donna nodded. "Yes, please. That way I can keep her arm stable."

"No ambulance?" Kylee asked.

"She doesn't want one," Donna explained. "I appreciate the offer, Cutter."

Kylee didn't know what to say or do.

"Brad's here. And they're sending up one of the students to help." Donna patted her hand. "They know how to do this—they all have to work emergency shifts. Don't worry."

"Kylee?" Shawn's voice was high, his anxiety clear.

"Come on back," Donna encouraged. "You can sit right here by your sister."

Shawn ran around the desk, sitting as close to her as he could. She placed a hand on his shoulder. "It's okay, Shawn. Fisher's back there. He'll take care of things." She meant it.

Mrs. Schwartz came out, her arm wrapped in gauze and plastic, leaning on a male student. Donna and Cutter led the way, helping the woman into Cutter's truck.

Kylee knew she had to keep calm. This was her job now. A good job she'd be an idiot to lose because of a ruckus. It wasn't like this was the first time she'd seen violence or blood—this was just a bad-tempered dog, not an abusive man. Besides, she couldn't leave without knowing Fisher was okay.

Somehow she managed to take care of the rest of the patients. If she wasn't sure of something, she jotted a question on a sticky note and attached it to the patient's paperwork. Brad left for the day but Cliff, the student sent to help her, knew where everything was and had answers for most questions. Still, she was relieved when five o'clock rolled around and the students assigned to emergency duty arrived.

She clocked out, then packed her notes and the manual into her backpack, glancing down the hall again and again. She wanted to poke around, to make sure Fisher was okay. But that wasn't her job and he wasn't hers to worry over.

"I guess tonight's off?" Shawn asked.

"I don't know," she answered, glancing at the clock. It was five fifteen. "Let's sit awhile. If Dr. Fisher is too busy, we'll walk home."

Shawn sat, trying not to look too disappointed. "Think he's okay?" he asked.

She nodded. "Definitely. I think Dr. Fisher could handle just about anything. Knowing him, he kept his cool and cracked a few jokes, too."

"Hey, Shawn, Kylee." Fisher sounded amused. "Ready to go?"

She was so relieved she didn't even try to hold back her smile. He was fine. She knew he would be, but…

"Yes, sir," Shawn answered.

"You two have fun." Kylee tugged up the strap on her backpack. "I have my shift tonight at Shots so I should head out."

He stood there, staring at her with a strange look on his face.

"I'm glad Goliath didn't eat you." She shook her head, trying not to get caught up in his gaze.

"You and me both," he answered, his gaze never leaving hers.

She tore her gaze away. "I'll see you tomorrow." Her breath was unsteady.

"Didn't Cutter take Mrs. Schwartz and Donna?" he asked. "You don't need to walk. I can drive you home, if you want."

She was nodding before she realized it. What was she doing? This was bad.

"How is Chance doing out at your place?" Shawn asked.

She loved that Fisher had adopted her little rescue dog. If she and Shawn had a more dog-friendly place, she would have brought Chance home in a heartbeat.

Fisher blinked. "You can see him yourself. I've been bringing him to work, getting him used to riding in the truck, playing with other animals and not chewing on the counters in my house." He laughed, leading them back into the hospital.

"How did your first day go?" he asked.

"Fine." She swallowed, all too aware of him.

"Things like today, with Goliath, don't happen often." He pushed open the door to Recovery. "Unless you're working emergency. Even then, people rarely get chewed up by their pets."

"What happened?" Kylee asked.

"Goliath wasn't happy to see me. We had him propped against a door so I could get some blood but Mrs. Schwartz was worried about him."

"She was *worried* about him?" Kylee shook her head. "Why not sedate him?"

"Owner's choice. If he's sedated he has to stay here until he's out of it—he's too big for her to carry into the house on her own." He shrugged, leading them between the kennels. "Anyway, she went to comfort him and Goliath bit her. I don't think he realized it was her or he wouldn't have done it."

Chance barked in greeting.

"He looks great," Kylee said, watching Shawn kneel and open the cage so the dog could run-hobble around her little brother in circles.

Shawn flopped onto the floor, laughing as the dog climbed into his lap and slathered him with doggy kisses. The carefree sound of her little brother was the best sound in the world. After everything he'd been through, it soothed her heart to see him laugh like the boy he was. She smiled up at Fisher. "Thank you." She paused. "For fixing Chance and…for making my little brother laugh."

Fisher nodded. His look was a little too intense…too much. She focused all of her attention on her brother, trying to contain the panic that fluttered wildly in her stomach. But it wasn't really panic; she knew panic. It was a sour feeling, a cold weight you couldn't shake. This was different. This was warm and sweet. And dangerous. Being close to Fisher was all it took to have her confused and…wanting. Her hands clenched against the slight tremor that ran down her arms.

She knelt beside Shawn, hoping her unease would lessen.

It had been a long time since she'd felt even a hint of interest in a man. Jesse was it. He'd been this handsome, charismatic guy offering to protect and care for her and

Shawn. It was less than a year before Jesse let her know she was his property—to do with as he pleased. She believed she deserved the abuse he rained down on her. And as long as Shawn was okay, she could endure it. In the end, she'd been patched and stitched up in almost every urgent care clinic and hospital in Las Vegas. If Miss Millie hadn't stepped in she'd probably be dead, and who knew what would have happened to Shawn.

Fisher wasn't Jesse. He was different. The effect he had on her was different. Fisher made her feel like a person, a person worthy of time and attention. He'd become her friend. Shawn's, too. She might think him handsome. She might worry over him. But she could never, ever, allow herself to form an attachment to this man.

"He's doing great," Shawn said, rubbing Chance behind his stubby ear. "You're the best, Dr. Fisher."

"I don't know about that, Shawn. If it wasn't for your sister, Chance wouldn't be here," he argued.

She glanced at Fisher then. It had never made sense to think in terms of *what if* or *I wish*, but right then Kylee wished with all her heart things were different. Yes, Fisher was her friend and she was thankful to have him. But there was a part of her, the what-if-I-wish part of her that wanted to let go and love Fisher with all her heart.

Chapter Eight

Kylee checked the neon illuminated clock over the bar for the tenth time in an hour.

Brook was here with Toben. And, from the way they were brushing up against each other and exchanging all-too-obvious looks, they were getting pretty close.

But Fisher and Shawn were still at the Boone Ranch.

She chewed the end of her pencil, trying to pay attention to the operations manual she'd brought home to study.

"What are you reading?" Cutter asked.

"Hey." She held up the thick black binder.

"You'll get the hang of it, Kylee. You've been there, what, two days?" Cutter smiled.

She shrugged, the sound of Brook's husky laughter drawing her attention. She frowned.

"What's up?" Cutter asked, peering around Kylee. "Who's that and why are you scowlin' at one of our customers?"

Kylee shook her head. "She's a surgical resident at the vet hospital." She didn't answer the second question. Cutter didn't need to know she was frowning because she was worrying about Fisher. She was frowning because he could walk in here any second and find Brook hanging on his cousin—and have his heart broken.

"She a bitch?" Cutter asked.

Kylee grinned at Cutter's directness. "No. She's nice."

"Uh-huh." Cutter nodded. "So this has something to do with Fisher Boone."

Kylee almost dropped her binder. "What?"

"I saw them in here a few nights back, cuttin' a rug and that redhead makin' eyes at Doc Fisher." Cutter crossed his arms over his chest and looked at her, waiting. "Course, I have cataracts so I could've been seein' things."

Kylee laughed. "I don't know what *makin' eyes* means, but yes, she and Fisher were here together last week." She shook her head. "I was hoping she and Fisher might get together."

Cutter made a dismissive noise. "And now she's here with Toben?" he asked. "Boy's got an eye for the ladies."

There was no disagreeing with that. "Maybe she doesn't know Fisher's interested?"

Cutter made the sound again. "Maybe?" He clicked his tongue. "Course *she* wasn't invited to the Boones for supper the other night, now, was she? Let me see…" He paused, scratching his chin. "No, I remember clearly it being me and Shawn and all the Boones…and you."

Kylee shot Cutter a look. "I know he likes her, Cutter."

"Oh, you do? He said as much?" Cutter waited, his brows arching in question.

He had. She sifted through their conversations…hadn't he?

"Uh-huh. Now, who'd he take on a tour of the Lodge? And whose little brother is he teaching to ride a horse?" Cutter poked Kylee in the shoulder with his finger.

Kylee stood there, listening to Cutter.

"Why are you so set on fixing him up with her?" He jerked his thumb in Brook's direction.

The lump in Kylee's throat made it difficult to say, "She'd be good for him. She's smart and funny and—"

"What about what he wants? I can tell you right now, it ain't that little redhead over there."

Why was Cutter saying this to her? He couldn't know that it hurt, to have her hopes and dreams put into words. She knew she and Fisher couldn't happen. "But—"

"No buts, Kylee. I might be old, but I ain't dead. That boy's only got eyes for you." Cutter nodded once. "I'm tired of seein' the two of you dance around it. When you get to be my age, you figure out you don't have as much time as you think."

She shook her head. "No, he doesn't." The lump seemed to get bigger. "I… She…"

"We brought burgers," Shawn announced as he sat at the bar, dropping two brown paper bags on the bar top. "And fries."

She jumped, so caught up in her conversation with Cutter she hadn't seen Shawn arrive…or Fisher, standing behind him. The air was officially knocked from her lungs when she saw Fisher. Instead of his usual snap-up plaid shirt, he was wearing a gray T-shirt. It showcased every ripple and angle of his muscles, stretched tight over his thick upper arms. He looked…and she felt…

This was the last thing she needed right now.

"Bring me anything?" Cutter asked.

"In the bag." Fisher was all smiles, until he saw her. "You okay, Kylee?"

She nodded, unable to avoid his green gaze. She knew Cutter was wrong, but…she wished he was right. She slammed her black binder shut and turned around, filling four cups with ice water. Her eyes burned and her chest felt heavy.

"You should have seen me," Shawn said.

"How'd it go?" Cutter asked.

"I rode a horse," Shawn said, the pride in his voice making her turn.

"You did?" She noted the flush on her brother's cheeks and the huge smile on his face. "Looks like you had a wonderful time."

Shawn nodded, accepting the ice water. "It was the best."

"He's got a knack," Fisher jumped in.

When she glanced his way he was still studying her. "Which one did you ride?"

"His name was Trigger," Shawn said.

Fisher sat on the bar stool beside her brother. "Trigger's a good horse. He and Shawn had that thing. That instant connection." He grinned.

Brook Marcus's laughter filled the bar.

"Sounds like someone's having a good time," Cutter said.

Kylee held her breath as Shawn and Fisher turned toward the pool table.

"When are we going bowling?" Shawn asked.

"How about next week?" Fisher said, turning back to the bar. If he was upset, there was no sign of it. She felt Cutter nudge her in the ribs, but she ignored him.

Fisher's gaze locked with hers. "You sure you're okay?"

Cutter picked up the manual. "Can't blame her if she's testy. She's been reading this thing most of the night. How's anyone supposed to read all those little, tiny words?"

"You have to learn all that?" Shawn asked, wrinkling his nose.

Fisher took the manual, flipping through it. "I'd be happy to help—"

"I've got it." She snatched the manual back and put it in the cabinet by the sink. She knew the three of them were staring at her, knew her eyes were stinging again and that she'd snapped at Fisher without provocation.

But everything Cutter had said was mixed up with everything she knew she shouldn't want and that kiss that should never have happened. She'd worried about Fisher, hurt for him, but he didn't seem to care that Toben had his arm around Brook. Or that Brook seemed perfectly happy to be manhandled by Toben. She was confused. She was tired. And she was tired of being confused.

"You should come with us next time," Shawn said, watching her.

"I have to work," she answered quickly.

"It doesn't have to be soon," Shawn argued. "I just think you'd like it."

"You're off this weekend," Cutter spoke up.

"I'm supposed to work—"

"No, now, Bobby called and said he needed the extra cash. He's got seniority." Cutter shook his head. "Besides, you've got two jobs now. You need a break, Kylee, or you'll end up downright crabby, like me."

Shawn reached over and took her hand. "We can do something after you get off work."

"Okay," she agreed. There was no way she could turn him down.

"We could go riding?" Shawn asked.

"We'll see," she murmured. "You guys can sit at a table and eat, if you want." Anything that would put space between her and Fisher—and that shirt.

Shawn and Cutter carried the food and drinks to a table, but Fisher stayed put.

"What's wrong?" Fisher frowned, concern lining his features.

She sighed, shaking her head. "It's been a long week."

"Agreed." He smiled at her. "Shawn had a really good time, Kylee. He's a natural cowboy."

"I'm okay with that. Well…as long as he's not a Mr. Belt Buckle kind of cowboy," she clarified.

He grinned. "And you thought *my* technique needed work."

Right. The technique she'd offered to help him with…

She looked at Brook, who looked ready to kiss Toben. Looked like it might be too late for Fisher. "I'm sorry about Brook," she said, searching his face.

He chuckled, the corner of his mouth tilting up. "You were the only one who thought we'd be good together."

She paused, sifting through his words. "You *would* be good together."

He cocked an eyebrow. "Kylee, I guess it's possible, but since neither one of us are interested, it's not really probable."

That lump was back in her throat again. "But…" She shouldn't think about the kiss. "You and I…" She shouldn't remember the way his hands felt against her face. "I asked you what you wanted to do…" She couldn't stop thinking about how good it felt to be in his arms.

He nodded. "You did." His jaw was clenched tight, the slight flare of his nostrils confusing her. "Did you ever stop to think that I did what I wanted to do?"

She shook her head, lowering her voice to an almost whisper. "You kissed *me*."

"Exactly." He gazed at her mouth. "And I've been wanting to do it again ever since."

Just like that, her world was upside down. His words were the most wonderful, terrifying thing she'd ever heard in her life. "You do?"

He nodded. "I'd like to take you out on a date, Kylee."

This was wrong, this was bad. He had to stop talking. Or she needed to walk away. Something. Anything to make this…this hope go away. Because hoping and wanting was dangerous—she knew that. But she also knew she'd never wanted anything the way she wanted Fisher Boone. And that meant losing him would be the worst thing ever. She shook her head. "No." She spoke clearly.

"No?" The corner of his mouth kicked up but there was no denying the surprise on his handsome face. "Just like that? So, you were fine when you thought I was kissing you to kiss Brook. But you won't let me kiss you?"

She leaned forward. "Can you keep your voice down, please?"

He leaned forward, too, so close to her she could see the shades of gold and brown in his eyes. It was getting very hard to breathe—to think.

"You didn't like kissing me, Kylee? Because I've thought about it every damn day since." His eyes bored into hers, his voice low and soothing—setting off all sorts of alarming tingles and shivers. "I don't know what you've been through but I know it was bad enough to make you cautious about things—"

"You're right," she hissed, desperate to stop him. Thinking about the past was hard enough. There was no way she'd talk to him about it. "You don't know. And

I'm glad. But I'm telling you right now, I'm not the right girl for you."

He was frowning now. "Why? Why won't you give me a chance?"

"I can't." She held up her hand, adding, "I can't do… this. I… People like you don't stay with people like me." She swallowed. "Shawn and I are figuring things out— on our own. We need to be on our own."

A memory of the Boones, of how close and supportive the family was, left her aching. Hope, doubt, happiness and grief—her emotions were all over the place. But one thing hadn't changed. She needed to hold on to that.

"You're a good guy, Fisher. Trust me when I say, you deserve better. My answer is no and that's not going to change. I mean it. So, please, don't ask again." She grabbed a tray and hurried off to clear tables before she said something she'd really regret. Something like yes.

FISHER WATCHED HER busing the tables. She moved with short, jerky movements, a crease between her brows and her mouth pressed tight. Why was she angry? He hadn't said anything that would get her riled up. Unless asking her on a date was offensive? He frowned.

"Good burgers," Cutter mumbled around his mouthful.

Fisher nodded, his gaze never leaving Kylee. She could be mad. Hell, *he* was mad. Why had she dismissed him so quickly? He knew she'd felt what he felt. He knew that kiss had affected her as much as it had affected him. Or maybe he'd just wanted that to be the case.

"She's tough," Shawn said.

Fisher looked at the boy. Shawn was watching his sister, a thoughtful expression on his face.

"What do you mean, she's tough?" Fisher asked.

"To figure out," Shawn explained.

He and Cutter nodded in agreement.

"Good worker," Cutter said. "Better sister than mine, that's for damn sure. Millie was a pain in my backside until she up and married Virgil Taylor and moved out of state. Never did understand why she and Virgil moved to the big city. He was always a do-gooder. Why he picked some place so far away to settle down is beyond me. Guess he thought he could do more good there."

"Miss her?" Shawn asked.

Cutter shrugged. "We talk on the phone. She sends me letters—still nagging me."

"I'd miss Kylee," Shawn murmured, popping several french fries into his mouth.

Fisher could understand that. He'd miss Renata if she ever left Stonewall Crossing. "You ever go visit her?" Fisher asked. He didn't know much about Millie, except she'd helped Shawn and Kylee. That made him a fan.

"Me? In Las Vegas?" Cutter's wheezing croak of a laugh spoke for itself.

"You and Miss Millie are a lot alike," Shawn said. "If it wasn't for her, we wouldn't be here. If it wasn't for you, we couldn't stay in Stonewall Crossing."

"You ever miss Las Vegas?" Fisher asked, curious. He and Shawn hadn't spent much time talking about anything other than horses. The boy had a quick mind. Once he'd learned something new, he was on to something else. But he, like Kylee, seemed wary of his past. He didn't want to push the boy, but he could sure use some insight into the woman he was falling for.

"Some of the people…*maybe*." Shawn shrugged. "But I know it's better here."

"Course it is," Cutter agreed.

Fisher caught Shawn's grin, noting the similarities between the boy and his sister. They had the same blue eyes and dark hair. But where Shawn was willing to smile and try new things, he knew Kylee struggled. He watched her long hair spill over her shoulder as she wiped off a tabletop.

"You like her? Want to date her…or be her boyfriend?" Shawn asked, drawing Fisher's attention. The boy's gaze was intent, searching. "My sister, I mean?"

Fisher looked at Cutter, then Kylee, then Shawn. He didn't lie, no matter what. And Shawn had asked him a direct question. Seemed like the best course of action was to give him a direct answer. "Yes."

"Thought so." Shawn nodded. "Is that why you're nice to me?"

Fisher almost choked on his water. "No." He stared at the boy. "You're a good kid. I have nephews. I have younger brothers." He shrugged. "There are things you want to learn and do that I can help you with."

Shawn nodded. "Making sure. A lot of times people are nice or do things because they're after something."

Cutter and Fisher exchanged a look.

"I guess they do," Fisher reluctantly agreed. "But I'm not being nice to you because I like your sister. I give you my word on that." He nodded, holding the boy's gaze. When Shawn nodded in return Fisher added, "But I guess it can't hurt." He grinned at Shawn, who smiled right back.

"Too bad she won't give you the time of day," Cutter teased.

Fisher scowled at him.

"I've never seen a fella try so hard," Cutter continued. "People here are different. The people we knew weren't like you. Kylee is sort of...*suspicious* because of that. She can't relax. She's still...ready all the time." Shawn's voice was low.

"Ready for what?" Fisher asked.

"To run." Shawn dropped the french fries onto his burger wrapper. "It was real hard. She...she had to take care of me. This guy..." Shawn's expression grew remote. Fisher had seen the same expression—almost a lack of expression—on Kylee's face more than once.

Shawn took a deep breath and continued, "This guy would help sometimes. When he needed something, he'd find us. A few times, he got us off the street and fed us— someplace. But he was real moody and had a bad temper. If Kylee or I did something wrong..." He broke off, shaking his head.

"He's the reason you two were in the state you were in when you got here?" Cutter asked.

Shawn nodded. "Kylee stood up to him, said she wouldn't do something. Jesse didn't like it when people told him no."

Fisher's blood was boiling so loud the roar in his ear was almost deafening. He stared blindly around the room, fighting the urge to react. Not that there was anything he could do about it but...

His gaze met Cutter's. The old man's face was fiery red.

"He was real protective, especially of Kylee. She couldn't talk to guys—unless he wanted her to." Shawn shrugged. "He was pretty cool with me."

Fisher sat back in his chair, digesting everything Shawn had shared. His hands itched, the urge to punch something overwhelming.

"She likes you, Fisher," Shawn said. "She doesn't talk

nice about anyone except you and Cutter." Shawn grinned at Cutter.

Fisher's heart turned over. "Guess that's a good start."

Shawn nodded. "Jesse said it's best not to get attached to something or someone because then you can get hurt." His blue eyes searched Fisher's. "Kylee's been hurt a lot, Dr. Fisher. Just so you know."

Those words twisted his heart, and his temper cooled until he felt cold—then numb. Kylee was keeping him at arm's length because she didn't want to get hurt again. How could he show her that was the last thing he wanted? If she couldn't love him, he still wanted to be her friend. He wanted to be Shawn's friend, too. From the sounds of it, the two of them had been facing the world on their own for a long time. It was time they had someone watching their backs.

"Sounds like she's got good reason to be scared of you," Cutter said to Fisher.

"Scared of me?" The words were a whisper, full of anguish. Was she really scared of him? He remembered the look on her face that night with George Carson. Maybe he did scare her. The idea made his stomach churn.

Shawn looked at his sister. "She doesn't know what to think of you. But she does talk about you a lot." He glanced at Fisher. "So, what are you going to do?"

Fisher frowned. "I'm not sure, Shawn. But I get the impression she might not want anything more than friendship."

"You ask her out yet?" Cutter asked.

Fisher sighed, nodding.

"Turned you down flat?" Cutter asked, cackling.

Fisher nodded again. "You don't have to sound so damned happy about it."

"I'm not happy about it," Cutter said, still grinning. "I might be a little tickled that you're going to have to work at this. It builds character, workin' for something."

"I've been working my whole life, Cutter, and you know it," Fisher cut in.

"Now, now, don't get your tail feathers in a knot, son. I know you work hard, that's not what I'm sayin'. But you've had it easy your whole life. You wanted something, you got it. I'm talking about workin' hard till you're bone tired and gettin' nothin' for it." Cutter spoke around a mouthful of burger. "I'm thinking that's what Shawn here's been talking about?"

"Yes, sir," Shawn agreed quietly.

"Makes sense Kylee might be a little shy about some big cowboy trying to court her. Especially after all they've been through." Cutter nodded. "I'm not sure you or I can understand what it means to struggle like they have."

Fisher sat there, bombarded by a wide range of emotions. Cutter was right. He couldn't do a damn thing about their past, no matter how much he might want to. But he would do what he could to ensure their future was better.

From the corner of his eye he saw Shawn drop a french fry on the floor, drawing his attention to the boy instead of the old man. He watched Shawn pick up the french fry, blow it off and eat it without thought. *Off the street and fed.* Fisher didn't really know what that was like— his life struggles had been few and far between.

He'd lost his mother when he was a teenager. It'd hurt like hell and put a wedge between his brother Ryder and their father that took years to heal. He remembered the long, heavy silences at the dinner table and his father's haunted look. Her absence had left a gaping hole, one that had never been filled or forgotten. But Fisher had never lost the safety of his family—or worried about losing the roof over his head or having food in his belly.

The loss and heartache he'd experienced was real, but even when things were at their darkest he'd had the love and support of his family. They might drive him crazy from time to time but he knew he could always count on them. A good portion of Stonewall Crossing, too, if need be. His life, his safety, his survival had never been at risk.

He knew that wasn't the case for Shawn and Kylee.

"I guess not," Fisher agreed, the realization so crushing it hurt to breathe.

Kylee.

His anger cooled, replaced by the aching warmth that only thoughts of Kylee stirred.

She was a fierce protector, a loyal sister and a survivor. She'd done what needed to be done, no matter what. Life on the streets…caring for Shawn…

He swallowed, trying to wrap his mind around what that meant. What that was like. He admired her strength and determination. And ached for what they'd never know.

His gaze sought her out. She was an amazing woman, he'd never doubted that. But maybe she didn't know that. If life had been as tough as he imagined for them, it was possible she'd never had the opportunity to be a woman— a woman in love, a woman given the love she so deserved.

Maybe it was time to change that.

Chapter Nine

Kylee sat behind the admissions desk, flipping through a stack of patient files. She'd made sure all the invoices and charts had been scanned into the database before putting them back into the manila files. If she had time, she'd file them before she went home for the day.

"Kylee?" Donna called her. "These are for you."

Kylee stood, coming to a complete stop when she saw the deliveryman—and the very large arrangement of flowers he held. "For me?" she asked, completely confused. "No—"

"Kylee James?" the man asked.

She nodded, reaching for the small envelope he held out to her. Her name was printed boldly across it. She signed on the deliveryman's clipboard, took the vase and set it on the counter, then opened the envelope.

"Who's it from?" Donna asked. "Those are the prettiest flowers. Just look at the colors."

Glenna was oohing over them, too. "Someone special we don't know about?"

Kylee shook her head, staring at the card. *Say yes*.

"Say yes?" Donna read over her shoulder. "Ooh, say yes to what?"

"That's all it says?" Glenna asked.

Tandy Boone's voice joined in with all the others. "Who got the flowers?"

But all Kylee could do was stare at the card. A card that was shaking in her hand. She dropped the card on the counter and left the desk, walking as sedately as possible into the women's locker room. All the students were on rounds, so she'd have some privacy—and there was a bathroom in the back where she could hide. And right now, she needed to hide.

By the time she reached the bathroom she was sniffling. She turned the handle but it didn't budge. She knocked, but there was no answer. She turned the knob again, rattling the door. She pressed her forehead against it, trying to calm down. Her eyes burned, her throat felt tight and her lungs were starving for air. But she knew one deep breath would push her over the edge and make her fall apart. She tried the door again, desperate.

What was he doing? Why was he pushing this? Didn't he understand? She wanted to say yes. But she couldn't… didn't he see the way things were?

"Kylee?" His voice was behind her. His wonderful voice, full of concern.

"Fisher…" She heard how high-pitched her voice sounded, how pathetic. She cleared her throat and tried again. "Women's locker room," she spoke, still facing the door. "You are not a woman."

"No, I'm not."

She almost smiled. Even now, with her eyes full of her tears and her heart torn, he could make her smile. "Go, please."

"Kylee." His hands clasped her shoulders. "Can you look at me?"

She shook her head, wishing his touch didn't affect her. "Can you leave?"

"Not until you look at me," he pleaded. "Please."

He'd go, and she could pull herself together and hope walking out hadn't cost her this job. She blinked several times, willing away the tears that made her vision blurred. She drew in a shaky breath, rubbed her nose with the back of her hand, straightened her shoulders and faced him. He was so…gorgeous.

"I'm sorry." There was no denying the sincerity in his voice. "I never meant to upset you." Standing there looking heartbroken, staring down at her with those big green eyes, she almost wanted to comfort *him*. She was making him feel this way? Act this way? It surprised her to see just how much her distress affected him.

She didn't understand him…but she wanted to. "Why did you send me flowers?"

"They made me think of you." He shook his head, his hands squeezing her shoulders.

She stared at him. Those beautiful vibrant flowers made him think of her? That made absolutely no sense. "I'm not playing hard to get, Fisher."

"I know." He frowned, stepping closer. "But, dammit Kylee, I'm not ready to give up on you—on us—yet."

She shivered, his words easing the pain in her chest. *Us.* He meant it. This was Fisher. He said what he meant. And what he said suddenly seemed more important than the mile-long list of reasons she had for telling him no. She didn't want to say no. She wanted him to pull her against him, she wanted his lips on hers. She didn't want him to give up. "You're not?"

He shook his head, pulling her—finally—into his arms. His eyes searched her face as his hand cupped her cheek and tilted her head back. But he didn't kiss her. He hesitated, so close she could feel his breath upon her skin. He was waiting for her, she knew that. If she stepped back, if she shook her head or turned away, he'd let her go. This was her last chance to stop him. Her heart was at risk.

But she didn't want him to let her go.

She closed the last inch between them, sliding her arms around his neck as his lips met hers.

His kiss was soft. And then it wasn't. Not because he was impatient, but because she was. She'd never had someone ask for her permission. She'd never had someone say sweet things to her. Or want her for her. She'd never had someone look at her as a woman instead of as an asset or a tool.

Fisher made her feel things—good things.

His tongue slid into her mouth, knocking her feet out from under her. But he had her, his strong arms holding her tightly to the wall of muscle that was his chest. He was strong, so strong, but he was also gentle. Her fingers slid through his closely cropped hair, cradling the back of his neck, and she reveled in the heat of his skin beneath her palm.

He ended the kiss with a groan, though his hold didn't ease. "Please go on a date with me, Kylee."

She couldn't think. Every cell was still sparking from the power of his kiss. She turned into him, her lips brushing his jaw. His scent reached her, making sure she was firmly caught up in one thing—Fisher.

"If you want, I'll kiss you again." His words were low and husky. His mouth met hers, his kiss lingering. "As much as you want."

As much as you want…

Her hands slid from his neck, down his shoulders, to rest on his chest. His hold tightened, making her look at him. And what she saw made something inside of her shift. For the first time in her life she understood what it meant to want a man's touch. She did. She wanted Fisher's touch. But, more than that, she wanted Fisher.

And she had no idea what to do about it. She'd never been this excited and anxious before. She didn't know how to act or what to say. What if she messed up? Did or said something wrong?

"I won't hurt you." His words rasped. "I will never hurt you."

And just like that, her eyes were burning and her chest ached. Not from pain, but from happiness. "I know," she whispered.

His fingers slipped through her hair. "I'm taking Shawn riding after work. Please come with us."

She nodded.

"That's not our date," he said, rubbing his thumb along her jaw.

"It's not?" she asked, surprisingly eager to get back to the kissing.

"Nope, it's a beginning." He pressed a kiss against her forehead. "I didn't mean to keep you. I just wanted to make sure you were okay. I am sorry about the flowers."

"Don't be," she answered. "I've never gotten flowers before."

His eyes narrowed, the shake of his head sharp. "That's a crime."

She smiled, wishing they could stay like this— wrapped up, just the two of them. But there was a clock on the wall over his shoulder. And in about two minutes, thirty college students would be coming in to hang up their coats and change. "I need to get back to work."

He nodded, but he didn't move.

"I should go," she tried again. But she wasn't prepared for the flare of panic she felt when he let her go.

He caught her hand in his, leading her from the dressing room. "I'll come get you around five thirty and we'll go get Shawn, okay?" he asked, walking her back to the admissions desk.

She tried to pull her hand away, but he held tight. The more she pulled, the bigger she smiled. "Isn't there some policy against dating coworkers?" she whispered.

He shook his head. "Nope. Only teachers dating students."

He squeezed her hand and headed back down the surgical hallway, leaving her to face Tandy, Donna and Glenna. The three of them all stood at the counter, openly watching and enjoying Fisher's little display of affection.

"Sorry about that," Kylee said as she headed back to the files she'd been holding. She tried not to smile at the vase overflowing with flowers. But she couldn't help it.

"No problem at all," Donna answered. "We all need a break now and then."

Kylee picked up the card and tucked it into her pocket.

"I'm guessing these are from my cousin?" Tandy asked, all smiles.

Kylee nodded, her cheeks going hot.

"Don't tell the others but," Tandy leaned closer, "Fisher was always my favorite cousin."

"I don't think I've ever seen Dr. Fisher smile like that before," Donna added. "And I've been working here long enough to know."

"Enough with the lovefest," Glenna spoke up. "I swear,

it's all flowers and smiles in the beginning. But it's going to be one awkward work environment after the breakup."

"Glenna," Donna scolded.

"Did someone wake up on the wrong side of the bed this morning?" Tandy asked.

Glenna shook her head. "Oh, come on." She shook her head. "I'm going to file these. It's getting a little too cutesy in here for me."

As Glenna disappeared around the corner, Donna said, "You better get used to that reaction, Kylee. I can tell you there are more than a few young ladies who were hoping to catch Fisher Boone's eye."

She didn't want the sweet happiness to fade. But Glenna's comments were a little too hard to ignore— especially since they were things she was already worrying about. What had she been thinking—to hold his hand, say she'd date him…? Nothing had changed. She was still the same person she'd been before he'd sent her flowers. Before he'd said *us*.

Except…when he held her in his arms, she wasn't thinking. Happiness took over. In his arms, that's what she found. And hope. And…want. Everything about Fisher was new and unexpected. And even though she knew she should be careful and keep her guard up, she was pretty sure it was too late to protect her fragile heart.

No matter how hard he tried to concentrate, Fisher couldn't stop thinking about Kylee. He'd spent the better part of the morning worrying over the flowers. He'd wanted to court her, to show her he was a gentleman— with good intentions. After listening to Shawn, he knew he had to take care. Kylee deserved hearts and flowers, romance and poetry. And he wanted to be the one to give that to her.

He'd known when the flowers were going to be delivered but when he'd made his way to the admissions desk he'd caught sight of her on the run.

"What's up?" he'd asked Tandy.

"These upset her." Tandy had pointed at the flowers. "Maybe I should go—"

"I'll go," he'd said, not waiting for an answer. He'd wanted to make her smile. Instead he'd made her cry.

Seeing those blue eyes shimmering with tears had torn his heart out.

And her kiss...

He swallowed now, focusing on the chart in front of him. He had to clear this chart before he could leave. In order to do that, and do it right, it was a bad idea to be thinking of the way Kylee's mouth tasted, of how her curves felt pressed against him or the sweet sound of her sigh.

He forced himself to check and recheck every line of the patient treatment care plan, then signed the bottom of the page. Another glance at the clock told him it had only been two minutes since the last time he'd checked.

Hunter had invited him to join his family at the bowling alley. If Kylee was interested and if Shawn got finished with his ride in time, it might be a good idea. Kylee might not want to spend too much time alone with him yet. He knew Shawn would want to go—he and Eli had hit it off.

Tripod jumped onto the counter, his purr loud and distracting.

"Hey, Tripod." Fisher rubbed the cat's black head,

smiling at the look of bliss on his face. "How's my favorite helper? Were you visiting Angelica?" he asked.

Angelica was a female cat that had been hit by a car. She was going to be okay, but she was pretty banged up and scared. She sat huddled in the far corner of her cage, mewing pathetically. Earlier he'd let Tripod into her cage and, after a fit of hisses and spitting, Angelica had quieted down. He'd peeked inside to see Tripod grooming the young calico.

"You're a good boy," he said, scratching the cat between the shoulder blades and along his spine. He glanced up to see Kylee in the doorway, watching him.

"You're talking to the cat?" Kylee asked. "And what is he saying?"

Fisher smiled at her. "He's pretty sure he's the coolest cat on three legs."

She giggled, rubbing Tripod's head. "Are there a lot of three-legged cats around here?"

Fisher pretended to cover Tripod's ears. "You don't want to hurt his feelings." He winked.

"This is the one? That cares for the other animals?" she asked, showering affection on the cat.

He nodded, watching her hand stroke Tripod. "He's an original," he murmured, caught up in the curve of her smile. "You ready to get Shawn?"

She nodded, her smile growing as Tripod flopped onto his back and exposed his belly.

"That's a sign of trust," Fisher explained. "Or he's daring you to rub his belly."

"Daring me?" she asked.

"You know, you touch my tummy and I'll bite you sort of thing." He shrugged. "Cats do that from time to time. They like to mess with people."

She looked at him then. "They do?"

He nodded. "They have an odd sense of humor."

She giggled. "I didn't know that."

He wanted to stroke the curve of her cheek. So he shoved his hands in his pockets instead. "Hunter's invited us to join them after Shawn's ride. Some bowling, maybe?"

"Maybe." She didn't sound enthusiastic, but it wasn't a no.

Tripod jumped down and trotted out of the exam room.

"Guess that means it's time to go?" she asked.

Fisher nodded. "You already speak pretty good cat."

He led her to his office so he could pack up his laptop and the stack of surgery assignments he needed to grade. Brook had taken half of them, so that left him with thirty-five papers to review.

"Homework?" she asked, staring around his office at the multitude of pet pictures and owner thank-you notes that Fisher had tacked up to decorate his walls.

"And here I thought I was done with school," he teased. "Good thing I love my job."

She turned, her blue gaze considering. "People respond to you—animals, too."

He almost dropped his bag on his desk, wanting to reach for her but worrying he was moving too fast. "Respond to me?"

She nodded, the intensity of her gaze holding him in place. Her reaction to him had been unforgettable. Would she respond the same way now? He couldn't test it. Shawn was waiting for him—no way he was going to disappoint the boy. So he finished packing up, turned off his office light and locked the door behind them.

"All those thank-you notes and drawings? All over

your office? I'm assuming they're from owners." She walked with him.

"Some are. Some are from the kids that come on field trips." He grinned. "We do a week each year for the surrounding elementary schools. We fix all sorts of torn and damaged stuffed animals for the kids, with a few stitches, some compression wrap and a couple of well-placed bandages. The kids love it. And me, too, of course."

She laughed. "I'm sure they have a great time."

He glanced at her, loving the sound of her laughter and the ease of her smile.

"Do you really think Shawn will be ready for the camp?" she asked as they made their way out of the school and across the parking lot to his truck.

He unlocked the passenger door and held it open for her. "I do."

She smiled, taking the hand he offered to step up into his truck. "Thank you."

"My sincere pleasure," he said, closing the door and walking around the front of the truck to get in. "Like I said, he's a natural rider. He and Trigger already have a solid rhythm. By the time camp starts, no one will be able to tell he's a beginner."

Their conversation centered on Shawn and the upcoming camp. He could tell she wasn't as excited over it as her little brother.

"Tell me what's worrying you so I can fix it," he said.

She looked at him. "About Shawn?" she asked.

That simple question made him pause. Would she tell him? Would she share the weight of all of her concerns with him?

"We can start there," he said.

"It's not a short list," she teased. But underneath the

light and airy tone of voice he suspected she wasn't teasing at all.

"Tonight, I'm all yours," he said, regretting the words the instant they were out of his mouth. He knew she was looking at him but couldn't look at her. "I mean, you have my undivided attention." When he did look her way, he was surprised to see a small smile on her face.

"I need to get him plugged in to something. He spends too much time alone for someone his age." She stared out the truck window. "In Vegas, we went everywhere together. But I can't bring him to work with me—I know that's not acceptable. Working at Shots can't compare to the vet hospital's pay or benefits, but Cutter doesn't mind if Shawn's around." She shook her head. "I don't know what to do with him, to keep him busy and out of trouble."

He didn't have an answer for her. He'd spent the long, hot days of summer running around with his brothers on the ranch. Most days his father had a list of chores he expected them to do. But once that was done, they'd climb trees, look for scorpions, skip stones on the lake or—if the water was high enough—tube down the river that ran through the ranch.

But Shawn was alone, in town. And there wasn't much for a twelve-year-old boy to do in a town the size of Stonewall Crossing. Unless…

"He could get a job," he offered.

Kylee looked at him. "I wasn't expecting you to fix anything, Fisher, I was just…talking."

She was talking to him. And he liked it, a lot. "I know. And I'm not trying to tend to your business. But I know Archer's been looking for some help at the animal rehabilitation center. He probably wouldn't pay Shawn, because Archer is Archer. But Shawn could volunteer there. Maybe a day or two there and another at the hospital. It can be dirty work, but it would definitely keep him busy. Until school starts in the fall. And he'd learn a lot about animals—and people, too."

They pulled in to Shots then and Shawn barreled into the truck, effectively ending the conversation. Instead of climbing into the back, Shawn squeezed in beside Kylee on the bench seat. That meant Kylee was flush against Fisher's side, knee to knee, thigh to thigh, hip to hip…

She stiffened instantly but slowly relaxed enough to lean against him. He didn't want to read too much into that. She was finally comfortable with him—that's all. It didn't mean she wanted his touch the way he craved hers. Did it?

Being so close to her, feeling the brush of her against him, made for one hell of a long drive. And he didn't mind one bit. He savored every second of the drive from town to the ranch and down to the barn. When they parked, Fisher had a hard time moving away from her. He was pretty happy to sit wrapped in her heat, her scent, with the air-conditioning blowing long strands of her hair against his neck.

He climbed out of the truck and glanced at her. She was sitting, her hands fisted on her knees, that look on her face. The look she'd had after he kissed her. The look that told him, maybe, her body was humming just as much as his. When their gazes collided, there was a palpable sizzle in the air. There was no denying the immediate effect she had on him. The desire to touch her was almost overwhelming. If Shawn hadn't been there, he'd have pulled her from the truck and picked up where they left off in the locker room. But Shawn *was* there, so Fisher winked at her instead. Her smile was huge.

"You going to ride, Kylee?" Shawn asked, coming around the truck to join Fisher.

She shook her head. "How about I watch."

Shawn nodded. "Will you try next time?"

Fisher waited, hoping she'd say yes. Shawn wanted to share this with her. It would be a good way to start making new memories together.

She nodded. "I will." She glanced down at her clothes. "Just remind me to put on some other clothes."

"Okay," he and Shawn said in unison, making her giggle.

A streak of gray and black came barreling across the yard and into Fisher's side. "How did you get out?" he asked Chance, who was dancing around on his back feet, eager for attention.

"Hey, Chance." Shawn knelt, all too happy to shower affection on the wriggling dog. "You an escape artist? Don't you know you're lucky to have this place for a home?" He held the dog's head between his hands. "You remember that and be a good dog for Doc Fisher."

The dog sat, his good ear perked forward, listening to Shawn. His stubby little tail wagged, he cocked his head to the side and he proceeded to cover Shawn's face with dog kisses. Shawn was laughing too hard to protest...

Seeing Shawn so carefree, laughing and smiling and acting like a boy his age should, made Fisher happy.

When Kylee's laughter joined her brother's, Fisher was pretty sure life couldn't get much better.

"I've been trying to teach him some manners," he finally said. "Chance, come on now, you're making me look bad."

Chance's ear perked up, then he ran to Fisher's side and sat at his feet.

"A little late now," he said to the dog, unable to not smile down at the animal.

"That's impressive," Kylee nodded at Chance. "He's listening to you."

"Sometimes," Fisher agreed.

"Sounds like he and Shawn have a lot in common," Kylee teased, hugging her brother with one arm.

Shawn grinned broadly. "You love me anyway."

Kylee kissed her brother's temple. "You know I do." Fisher caught the look she gave her brother, so full of love there was no way the boy could doubt it.

Shawn sighed, shrugging out from under her arm. "I think I'll go get the saddle and gear together."

"You know where it is." Fisher nodded, pleased Shawn was so excited over his riding time. Shawn headed straight for the barn. Chance was at his heels, ear quirked up and ready for direction.

Fisher's attention returned to Kylee.

She was looking at him. "Thank you," she said, walking the short distance that separated them. She stared up at him, so beautiful and tempting he didn't know which was better—looking at her or kissing her. With Shawn in the barn, he decided to keep his hands to himself. But it wasn't easy.

He swallowed against the lump in his throat. "For what?" His voice was gruff.

"For caring about Shawn," she murmured, placing a hand on his chest. "For showing him he's worthy of your time."

His hand covered hers. "He is." He paused. "And so are you, Kylee." His fingers threaded through hers, pressing her palm over his heart. "I want to spend more time with you."

She drew in a deep, unsteady breath. "I'm here."

Fisher lifted her hand and kissed her palm. "I'm glad. Having you here feels right. I hope it becomes a regular occurrence." Maybe he shouldn't be so forthright with her. But when they were alone together he opened his mouth and all his thoughts and emotions tumbled out, unfiltered and raw.

"Fisher…" She broke off, her eyes searching his. "I… I don't know what to say."

"You don't have to say anything." He held her hand and set off toward the barn. "Shawn's probably waiting on us. He and Trigger are off to a real solid start. Shawn's a natural cowboy." He glanced at her. "Not the big-belt-buckle type."

Chapter Ten

Kylee was amazed. Shawn looked like he'd grown up in the saddle. Every day he got better. His lean frame swayed in time with the horse's rolling gait. She didn't know how she felt about the pace they were going, but Shawn seemed nothing but happy.

Happy.

She'd never expected that to be a regular part of her life. But in the week since Fisher had sent her those flowers it had been there, waiting for her. Happiness. It was Fisher, she knew that.

She'd never had a man want to know her the way he did. It wasn't about sex, though she could tell he was interested. It was more than that. It was the way he offered an encouraging word when she was working at the vet hospital. The warm, yet always respectful way he treated her in public. Like she was his equal, not his inferior. And the way he worked to make her laugh.

She'd only just realized it, but something about her laugh made him stand up straight with pride. She didn't want to admit she was in love with him—that was beyond her reach. Whatever this bone deep ache and sweetness was, she knew she didn't want it to end.

Shawn waved at her as he and Trigger galloped by. Fisher was on Waylon, at Shawn's side to spot her brother.

There were times she still couldn't believe they were here, safe and…happy. If Miss Millie hadn't loaded them onto that bus, where would they be? Jesse had told her she was going to work for Mr. Fox doing things she didn't want to think about and Shawn was staying with Jesse. She'd told him no and ended up in the emergency room.

Mr. Fox wasn't a street criminal like Jesse, he was bigger—scarier. Mr. Fox had a legendary temper, treating his employees like property. Her life with Jesse wouldn't seem so bad in comparison to working for Fox.

She crossed her arms over her chest, a chill racking her body and covering her arms with goose bumps. That was over. She was lucky. They were lucky. She was here… with Shawn.

"What do you think?" Shawn asked, slowing Trigger in front of her.

"I think you look good," she said, shading her eyes against the fading sun. "I'm impressed."

"I know, isn't it cool?"

She nodded.

"Fisher's been great," Shawn said. "He's real patient. He doesn't yell or anything."

She glanced at Fisher and saw the quick frown on his face. He recovered, a smile in place when Shawn turned to look at him.

"Doc Fisher is great," she agreed, meaning it.

Fisher tipped his hat to her then, the gesture so old-fashioned and charming she couldn't stop herself from smiling.

"Can I walk him around the arena a few times?" Shawn asked Fisher. "I'll go slow."

"Sure," Fisher said.

Shawn moved away, letting Trigger amble along the fence line.

"You were right," she said.

Fisher nudged Waylon closer. "About what?" he asked.

"He's really good," she said, patting Waylon's neck.

Fisher's attention wandered beyond her, making her turn around. Hunter, his wife, Josie, and Eli were heading over from the barn to the corral.

"Nice to see you, Kylee," Josie said, smiling brightly. "Shawn looks great on Trigger."

Kylee nodded. "He's loving it."

"We thought we'd stop by. They're playing a movie on the courthouse lawn tonight." Hunter said. "Eli really wants Shawn to come."

"Can he spend the night?" Eli asked.

Hunter smiled. "We'd like to invite Shawn back to the house for an overnight, too, if that won't interfere with any plans."

She paused. Shawn had never spent the night away from her—ever. But maybe he should. If he wanted to, she should let him. It was all part of a normal childhood, wasn't it? Sleepovers, bowling with friends, having a good time.

"If he wants to," she agreed, trying to sound like it was no big deal.

"I'll go ask him," Eli said, already heading across the corral to Trigger and Shawn.

"You two want to join us?" Hunter asked.

"Or Fisher could make her dinner." Josie glanced at her husband. "Give Kylee a break. Archer's helping your dad at the Lodge, so it'll be a break for you, too, Fisher."

They all laughed then.

She and Fisher, alone. No interruptions. Just the two of them. They'd had a few stolen kisses but they were rarely alone. The last thing Kylee had expected to feel was anticipation. But she did. At the same time, she didn't want to presume that Fisher wanted—

"Sounds like a plan," Fisher said.

Twenty minutes later the horses were in their stalls, Shawn was packed into Hunter's truck and Kylee was standing in Fisher's living room. She'd spent some time here during the last week, when Shawn was riding. That Fisher had built the stone-and-wood house with his family made it even more impressive. With its vaulted ceiling and a carved wood mantel over the fireplace against the back wall it was both homey and dramatic. They'd played some cards, eaten some incredible stew and biscuits Fisher had made for them, enjoyed toasting marshmallows in the fireplace with the rest of his family and were still working on a huge puzzle of a herd of galloping horses. In one short week, she had come to love being here—with Fisher.

Her fingers traced the intricate wire frame of a table lamp. The bold black steel looked like recycled wagon wheels, horseshoes and other farming implements.

"Archer does that," Fisher nodded.

"He made this?" she asked, bending to study the metalwork.

"When he's not avoiding people or healing animals, he's welding furniture out of cast-off farm and ranch equipment." Fisher shrugged. "Can't accuse him of being lazy."

She smiled. *Lazy* wasn't a word she'd apply to any of the Boones. "Your family is incredible. Must be nice to be a Boone."

He nodded. "It is. I'm lucky, they're good people."

She nodded, immediately caught up in the pull of his green eyes. It didn't seem to matter that a couch and two tables lay between them, their connection was undeniable. The more time they spent together, the stronger it became. Especially when they were alone, like they were now. She wanted to go to him…but she couldn't move.

He did. He came closer, and his hands settled on her shoulders, his thumbs trailing the ridge of her collarbone. How could such a light caress make her breathless? How could such a big man look at her with such tenderness?

"Kylee." Her name rumbled from his lips.

"Fisher," she said, her hands clasping his forearms. His heat filled her, warming her until her stomach was molten and heavy and aching.

"I'm going to kiss you." He was still asking for her permission. And her heart melted.

She nodded, running her hands up his arms to grip his shoulders. The cotton of his shirt did little to cover the expanse of his shoulders. His shoulders were thick, as was the rise of muscle along his neck. He was a strong man, a man who could be considered dangerous.

His kiss was firm, his lips melding with hers. One hand cupped the back of her head, the other twined about her back to hold her flush with his chest. She could feel his heart thundering, echoing her own.

"This is where you belong. In my arms," he whispered against her ear.

She wanted to agree, but all she could do was hold on to him. His lips latched onto her earlobe, making her startlingly aware of every inch of her body. She throbbed with something she'd never experienced before. When his lips and tongue trailed along the line of her neck, she slid her arms around his waist—seeking some sort of anchor.

His lips traveled along her jaw, but it wasn't enough. She turned into his kiss, her lips parted in invitation. Fisher's kiss... He kissed her in a way that blotted out the world. It was just her, held in his strong arms, pressed against this mountain of a man who cared about her.

His tongue touched hers, eliciting a groan from him and a gasp from her. He stopped suddenly, resting his forehead against her own. Her fingers gripped the back of his shirt, wanting to keep him where he was...needing him to stay. But his arms relaxed and he stepped away from her, the look in his eyes revealing just how conflicted he was.

"You're being careful with me?" she asked, surprised at how husky and ragged she sounded.

He nodded once, his gaze falling to her lips.

She swallowed her nerves. "I know you won't hurt me. Kiss me, Fisher," she said.

His jaw clenched briefly before he crushed her against him. His mouth was demanding and she didn't mind. She deepened her kiss, gripping his head with both hands and standing on tiptoe to hold on to him. Her scrubs top moved with her, partially exposing her back and midriff. His hand was like a brand against her skin, rocking her to her core. She shuddered, the heat of his skin on hers powerful. She ached, wanting more. His kiss eased, his lips a featherlight caress as his hand slid beneath her shirt along her spine.

His hand shook. His breath hitched... Because he was touching her. Because she affected him, the way he affected her. Her heart thumped, stunned that she could make anyone feel something so powerful. She was glad it was Fisher. She clasped his face between her hands and stared up at him. His green eyes were foggy with desire, something she'd never known before. But now…she desired this man. And she loved him.

His hand moved down her spine and along the waist of her pants. When his fingers traveled upward, she shuddered. His palm was pressed against her side while his fingers stroked the flesh along her bra's edge.

His hand disappeared and he stepped away from her. "Damn, I'm sorry, Kylee." He ran a hand over his face. With another shake of his head he marched out of the room to reappear on the other side of the bar that separated the large family room from his kitchen.

She was still standing there, reeling, when he started rummaging through the kitchen cabinets. What was happening? She hadn't stopped him…she hadn't wanted him to stop. She still didn't want him to stop. Whatever he'd triggered inside of her, she wasn't ready to let it go.

"Chicken?" he asked tightly, staring into his refrigerator.

She stared at him, unable to rein in the sensations he'd stirred.

He looked at her, almost apologetically.

"You're hungry?" she asked, trying to make sense of his reaction.

He closed the refrigerator door deliberately, his hands resting on his hips. "I figure now's a good time to put some space between us." His voice was low, his tone controlled.

She frowned. "Why?"

He shook his head, his breathing still irregular.

"What…did I do something wrong?" she asked, confused by his behavior. "If… I can go."

"No. It's me. I'm pushing things, pushing you." He placed both hands on the counter, leaning forward. "I don't want you to go. I want you to stay. But I invited you for *dinner* and I meant it. I wasn't trying to get you into bed."

His words made her heart thump. Knowing Fisher, that was probably true. She'd never thought she'd be interested in being in Fisher's bed. But now it sounded like the perfect place to be. "You...you don't want to sleep with me?" she asked.

He stared at his hands on the counter, the muscle in his jaw leaping. "Kylee...hell, I want you to love me." He broke off, looking at her. "Like I love you. Because I do. I love you." His jaw muscle jumped again. "I want you. I want you so bad I hurt. But you need to know I'm not just in this for sex. I'm in this for you. And me. And the future I want with you."

He loved her. He, Fisher Boone, loved her. She'd never heard anything more wonderful. At the same time, it made no sense. How could someone like him love her? "You can't love me, Fisher," she argued. "Not after the things I've done. I'm not—"

"I can love you, Kylee James, and I do." His eyes swept over her. "I may not know every detail of your life before Stonewall Crossing but it doesn't matter. You did what you had to so you could take care of you and Shawn. I respect that. I respect you. I love your gentle heart. Your fierce loyalty. You're a beautiful—good—woman. And whether or not you want to argue about it, I *do* love you." He pushed off the counter, turned back to the refrigerator and pulled the door open.

She smiled. She didn't want to argue about it. She wanted to believe him. She knew, in her heart, she knew she was his. Whatever happened, there was no point denying it. She didn't want to deny it. He didn't judge her. He respected her. He loved her. And he didn't want to push her into doing something she didn't want to do.

What he didn't understand was that she did want this, all of this. All of him.

She moved around the bar and into the kitchen. She slid her arms around his waist, holding on tightly as she said, "I love you, too, Fisher." She paused, digging deep for the courage to say, "I love you. I don't want dinner right now. I want you."

He froze briefly.

And then she was cradled in his arms and being carried up a flight of stairs. She'd only just slid her arms around his neck and buried her nose against his neck when they entered his bedroom.

He had a big bed. But then, Fisher was a big man. The brown sheets were a tangled mess, the blankets hung halfway off the mattress. "I wasn't expecting company," he murmured as he set her feet on the floor.

She looked up at him. "Sorry to change your plans."

"I'm not." He smiled down at her, running a hand through her hair. "You sure?"

She nodded, despite all of her insecurities bubbling up. "I… I've never been so sure."

He shook his head, dropping a kiss on her lips. Even now, he seemed hesitant, like he was holding back. His eyes met hers, his hands cupping her face as he inspected every inch of her face. "I love you." His words shattered any lingering doubts she had.

She slid her arms around his waist. "Then kiss me."

His mouth was magic. He kissed her so long and deep that she was only vaguely aware of their clothes disappearing. When they fell onto the bed, she didn't know. But the electric shock of his chest against hers was exhilarating. She opened her eyes; her fingers stroked the muscled contours of his body. They lay, facing one another, a bedside lamp casting a warm glow in the room.

How could she have imagined a man could look like this? His arms were thickly cut, the raw strength of his body reassuring. His strength would protect her. He was rugged and hard and beautiful. She let her eyes explore him, the physicality of his body heightening the thrum of want in her blood. This man loved her and wanted to make love to her.

She looked at him, surprised to see him watching her face. His smile was gentle, but his locked jaw revealed just how much he wanted her. And she wanted him, so much. She lifted his hand and placed it on her side. "Touch me?"

FISHER HEARD THE uncertainty in her voice and reacted instantly. It didn't matter that he was barely in control, that just lying at her side was affecting him in a way he'd never expected. If she wanted him to touch her, he would touch her. Every soft, sweet inch of her. He didn't know where to start. Full breasts, a narrow waist, and flared hips—he swallowed—her body was made for touching, for kissing and loving.

He was glad he'd turned on the bedside lamp. He wanted to see her, he wanted to take his time to love every inch of her. His gaze followed the path of his fingers as he stroked along her ribs. She had an oval birthmark on the top of her right hip…

He stooped and kissed the small oval. His hand slid up, his lips dropping kisses along the curve of her side, his palm resting on her chest, fingers and thumb cradling the weight of her full breast.

Kylee. In his heart and his bed. She loved him. And trusted him.

He bent forward, sucking the rosy tip into his mouth. Her fingers gripped his head tightly, the sound she made in the back of her throat driving him mad. His tongue traced and circled, his lips tugged and sucked, making her moan as she arched into him—asking for more. Her responsiveness was all the encouragement he needed. He moved over her, easing his knee between her legs. His hands cradled her face as he kissed her.

He moved slowly into her, trying not to lose himself in her tight heat. She clung to him, her thighs pressed against his hips and her hands gripping his back. She shifted beneath him, the sweet friction too much. One hand moved to her hip, holding her still until he gained control.

"Fisher—" Her voice was broken.

His eyes met hers and held. He moved, sliding deep—forcing himself to keep a slow and steady rhythm. He wanted to watch her, soak in her every sigh and moan. Seeing her fall apart was powerful. The shift of emotions on her face, the way her body tightened and trembled around him, the desperate cry that spilled from her lips as she held tightly to his hips. His climax was fierce, shattering him and leaving him shaken.

He stared down at her, smiling at her flushed cheeks and the rapid rise and fall of her chest. Which drew his attention to her breasts. "Damn beautiful." He stooped, leisurely kissing the tip of one, then the other.

Her fingers slid through his hair, and she laughed softly.

He propped himself on his elbows and looked down at her. "Am I crushing you?"

She shook her head, her breathing calming. Her fingers ran along his hairline, the bridge of his nose and his mouth. "You're handsome."

He caught her hand and kissed it. "I am."

She laughed then, shaking her head.

"That is the sweetest sound in the whole world," he said, still holding her hand.

She shook her head again.

"It is. I know it is," he said, threading his fingers with hers. "I'd be willing to bet Shawn would agree."

"He's biased," she argued.

"He's not the only one." He stooped, dropping a kiss against her parted lips before rolling onto his back. He glanced at her, staring up at the ceiling, clutching the sheet to her chest. "Come here," he said, sliding his arm beneath her and pulling her against his side.

She sighed, melting into him. Her hand rested on his chest; her fingers stroked slowly back and forth.

"I like being here."

"I love having you here," he confessed. "I hate taking you home."

She looked up at him. "You do?"

He nodded. "Worst part of my day," he murmured. "Guess I should give you an actual tour?"

She rested her chin on his chest and looked at him. "Maybe later?"

He nodded, rubbing his hand up and down her spine. "Donna said you've already got the hang of things at work. You happy at the vet hospital?"

"She's just being nice." Kylee smiled. "I wish she wasn't leaving."

He smiled. "She won't be far. She lives a few blocks from Shots. Knowing her, she'll be glad to come in and help if you ever need her."

"You know everyone in town?" she asked.

"Pretty much."

"Must be nice to live in a place that makes you happy. I can't imagine ever leaving."

Her words made his heart swell. He never wanted her to leave.

"I did leave," he admitted. "I served as a military dog handler and then as a veterinarian. I went all over the place. And every day I missed home."

"You're so close to your family—that must have been hard."

"I had a friend with me," he paused. "Vince was like another brother."

"Where is he now? You two still close?"

"We talk a couple of times a month. He's in Florida. He runs a boxing gym. Wife, three kids." He smiled. "He's living it up."

"Boxing?" Her eyes narrowed. "Were you a boxer?"

He nodded. "Until I put Vince in the hospital. After that, I do my best never to lose my control."

She stared at him, her blue eyes unflinching. "He's okay?"

Fisher nodded. "A couple of weeks it was pretty touch-and-go. Once he pulled out of the coma, he wanted to get back in the ring." He shrugged.

"That must have been hard on you. I'm glad he's okay. And I'm glad it didn't cost your relationship. Accidents can do that." Kylee studied him for a long time. "Never miss boxing?" she asked.

He shook his head. He meant it. He kept busy, stayed

in shape. But he knew he'd never get enjoyment out of boxing the way he once had.

"I'm glad you came back to Stonewall Crossing." Her hand rested on his upper arm. "If you hadn't, I might never have met you."

He nodded, cupping her cheek and pulling her close to press a long kiss against her mouth. He was right where he needed to be, holding her—loving her.

She was settled in at his side when she added, "I never thought I'd end up in a place like this."

"You saying you're disappointed?" he asked.

She pressed a kiss to his chest, her arms tightening about his waist. "No. Surprised, maybe."

"Where did you think you'd end up?" he asked.

She glanced at him. "I gave that up when I was little."

"Gave what up?" he asked, wrapping a long strand of her black hair around his finger.

"Playing the what-if game. It can be defeating." There was no inflection to her words. "It's better to take one day at a time—have no expectations."

He stared up at the ceiling overhead, asking, "What happened, Kylee? How did you and Shawn get here?"

She lay there, her fingers stroking along the plane of his stomach, without saying a word. He'd almost decided to change the subject when she spoke, her words so rushed he knew it was hard to tell him.

"Shawn was born, dad died and suddenly we had no money, house or car. Mom worked all the time, but we struggled." She paused. "Shawn kept me and Mom going. He never cried, even when he was a baby."

She drew in a deep breath, her pace slowing. "Mom went missing my freshman year of high school. It took a few weeks to learn she was dead—assaulted and left in a field. We had no one so we started bouncing through foster homes. Some okay, others weren't. I was almost ready to graduate when they said I'd have to leave the system…and Shawn."

In that instant, Fisher understood. There was no way she'd ever leave Shawn undefended.

"I was too young to be his guardian. And the home we were in then…" She shook her head. "I didn't know what I was going to do, but I couldn't leave him. The night of my graduation, we took the bus from Oregon to Las Vegas. Jesse was waiting at the bus station, looking for kids like Shawn and me—young, scared, impressionable. Stupid."

"You were taking care of your brother, Kylee, protecting him," Fisher argued.

"But I didn't," she spoke softly. "He's a good pickpocket. He can hotwire a car. He can swipe a phone, a set of keys, even a purse without getting caught." She paused. "He's twelve, Fisher…but he's not. Sometimes I worry he'll never really be a kid. Because of me he lived on the streets—without Jesse, we were eating out of dumpsters, sleeping in cardboard boxes and begging for money. Jesse might not have had the best intentions, but he got us off the streets. Something I couldn't manage to do for my little brother."

His heart hurt—for her, for Shawn. At the mention of Jesse, something hot and hard settled in the pit of his stomach. He wasn't a vengeful man, but he suspected he'd get great satisfaction from punching the man senseless. "I wish I could make it better."

She looked up at him. "It's getting better. I just hope one day Shawn doesn't wake up and realize I'm the reason his life was so messed up."

"You're not. What alternative did you have? Leave him?" Fisher frowned. "He loves you, Kylee. I think you're his hero." He smoothed her hair back. "He's a kid. They bounce back. And the Shawn I know is happy."

"That's all I want—for him to be happy."

"What about what you want?" he asked. She'd spent so long worrying over Shawn's well-being, their very survival. Did she know what she wanted? Did she know there was nothing holding her back now?

"I don't want anything."

"Nothing?" he asked, cocking an eyebrow.

She studied him again. "All I ever wanted was love— maybe for Shawn and me to be part of a family." She looked at him, hesitant. "Over time, I knew that wasn't going to happen."

He sat up, gripping her shoulders. "Kylee—"

She placed a hand over his mouth. "Then I met you." She drew in a shaky breath. "After everything I've been through, I should know better than to hope. I should know better than to listen to my heart. But you say things, do things, that…that make me hope again."

Her words gutted him. "You've got a second chance in Stonewall Crossing, Kylee. You and Shawn. I want to be a part of that, a big part of that, if you'll let me. But, whatever you want, I'll help you get it."

She shook her head, her long hair rippling around her shoulders.

"What?" he asked, pulling her closer.

"Why me?" she whispered.

"Why not you?" he asked, tilting her head back to peer into her blue eyes. "I love you because of who you are. Considerate, protective, fierce, cautious." He stroked her cheek. "Patient, smart, loyal." He kissed the tip of her nose. "Gorgeous, kind and sexy."

She laughed. "You're only saying that because I'm naked."

He shook his head. "No, I'm saying it because it's the truth. Though I admit I do appreciate your nakedness."

"No one's ever talked to me like you do. Or cared what I thought or felt. Or looked at me—with that look right there." She tugged her sheet up.

"I like looking at you," he said with a grin.

"No one's ever seen me naked," she added. "No one's ever touched me the way you have. Or loved me enough to show me sex shouldn't be an obligation or a cold act. With you…" She swallowed. "You make my body respond…lose control…and fall apart."

He swallowed. She'd never had a man worship her body, never known what pleasure was…never had the love of a man. "It's because I love you. I want to touch you, to kiss you, to make you fall apart in my arms—so I can catch you and love you all over again."

"I want to fall apart with you," she murmured as she reached for him. Her lips met his and she let the sheet drop, wrapping her arms around him and holding him close. How he'd managed to gain this woman's love, he didn't know. But he'd make damn sure he did everything he could to keep it.

Chapter Eleven

Kylee opened her eyes to the sun streaming in the window. Fisher lay at her side, his arm and leg draped across her and holding her in place. She smiled, too happy to move. She'd spent the night but there hadn't been much sleeping.

"You awake?" His voice was muffled against her shoulder.

"Yes," she whispered. "Are you?"

He chuckled. "I'm not sure. I'm pretty comfortable."

She hugged the arm he had wrapped around her.

"But I smell pancakes," he said. "And bacon."

She froze. "You do?"

He nodded against her shoulder. "Probably Archer."

"Archer?" she repeated.

He looked at her. "What's wrong?"

She shook her head.

He grinned. "You embarrassed?"

She grinned back. "No…maybe… I don't know." Her stomach growled. "But I am hungry."

"You were the one that kept saying you weren't hungry," he argued.

"I wasn't last night. But I'm starving now."

He stretched, shifting his weight off her. "Let's go eat."

She rolled onto her stomach to watch him. She'd been amazed at how quickly her inhibitions had gone out the window. She was just as fascinated by his body as he was with hers. Every ridge and crease of his abdomen, the taper of his hips, the broad expanse of his chest... she liked looking at him—and the effect looking at him had upon her.

She headed for the shower, trying not to giggle or squeal when he climbed in beside her. He washed her hair, scrubbed her back and had a little too much fun with the washcloth. He tossed her one of his shirts and a pair of drawstring shorts. They were both too big, but they were clean.

He showed her around. The stairs led into a large room lined with books and family photos as well as a large stone fireplace and desk. Fisher referred to it as his office. On the other side of the room were two more bedrooms and another guest bath.

The best part of the space was the open wall. It gave the office the look and feel of a loft, and allowed them to peer down into the living room below.

She followed Fisher down the stairs and slammed into his back.

"Morning, *everyone.*"

Everyone? Should she run back upstairs? There was no way she'd get there undiscovered.

"Morning," Archer said. "I made breakfast."

"You picked a hell of a day to sleep in," another voice joined in. "I'd like to get this over with. I don't like leaving Annabeth alone all that long."

Annabeth. Kylee remembered her. Sweet, pretty, very pregnant. Chances were this was Ryder.

"She's probably grateful for the break," another voice said. Probably Hunter.

She sucked in a deep breath. Looked like she was going to be having breakfast with the whole Boone family.

"Would have been nice if someone let me know what was happening," Fisher said.

"I did," Archer argued. "I sent you a text."

Fisher sighed.

"Eat," Archer continued. "The water pipe isn't going to fix itself."

"Coffee's in the kitchen," someone said.

Fisher turned, giving his head the slightest shake before he asked her, "You want some coffee?"

She nodded.

"Kitchen's this way," he said, taking her hand and pulling her after him.

"You're out of creamer," Renata said as Fisher came into the kitchen. And then she saw Kylee. "Well, good morning." She was all smiles. "I'm guessing you didn't get Archer's text?"

Kylee accepted the mug Fisher offered her. She knew Fisher's brothers were staring at her, but there wasn't anything she could do about it. Except be absolutely delighted that finding a woman with Fisher was an uncommon occurrence.

There was a skillet of eggs, a tower of tortillas, another skillet with potatoes, and a mountain of bacon and sausage on a plate. Her stomach grumbled again. When was the last time she'd eaten?

"Can I do anything?" Kylee asked.

"No," Archer answered. "There might be enough for you, if you're hungry."

Fisher smacked him on the back of the head. "She's my guest, Archer, so try to be nice." He handed her a plate. "Help yourself, Kylee."

She took it, warming at the affection on his face. "Thank you."

He winked at her.

"You two are a little too chipper this morning," Ryder said. "I need more coffee."

Kylee made her plate, went around to the other side of the bar and sat on the last bar stool. She watched the brothers serve themselves, shoving and pushing and acting like kids.

"I don't think they ever grow up." Renata sat beside her. "Nice to see you."

Kylee smiled.

"Shawn had a good time last night," Hunter said, eating his breakfast taco while he leaned against the counter. "He taught Eli how to play poker."

Kylee's smile dimmed. "He did? He shouldn't—"

"We played for gummy bears and he won." Hunter smiled. "The gummy bears were Jo's idea so don't blame me if his stomach hurts. I'm pretty sure he and Eli ate them all."

She laughed, knowing her little brother was a card shark. "Thank you," Kylee said.

"He's a good kid." Hunter nodded. "He said you raised him so you get the credit for that. Jo can bring him home around eleven if you want."

"Thanks." She felt Fisher at her back and glanced up at him.

"Get enough?" he asked.

She nodded. "Sounds like you've got some work to do. I should go anyway. It's laundry day." She regretted it as soon as the words were out of her mouth. She didn't want to leave. She didn't want to go home. She wanted to stay here, with Fisher...

"Might want to change first," Fisher said in her ear. "Take my truck. When you come back we could take Shawn for a ride, explore the ranch a little?"

She nodded. "I'd like that."

Ten minutes later the kitchen was clean and the Boones were filing out his front door, waving their goodbyes. Fisher waited until they were alone before he wrapped his arms around her. She stepped closer, slid her arms around his waist and her hands beneath his shirt. "I'm sorry I have to run out on you this morning."

"Me, too," she admitted.

He kissed her, then again, his lips lingering until she opened for him. He groaned, crushing her against him. He pressed his keys into her hand as he broke away from her. "I'll make you and Shawn dinner tonight," he promised.

She smiled. "Okay."

He paused just inside the door. "I'm glad I'm coming home to you." And then he was gone.

Kylee stared at the door, smiling. His words warmed her from the inside. And even though he'd just left, she couldn't wait for them to be together again.

She poked around, exploring the house while she enjoyed a second cup of coffee. There was another room downstairs. It looked like an office, but there was a pullout bed in the couch that was in use. Probably where Archer was sleeping.

She headed back upstairs and made the bed, smoothing the blankets and fluffing the pillows. His was soft, holding his scent. She buried her nose, breathing him in deeply. When the pillow was back in its place, she folded up her clothes and headed out to Fisher's truck. It was a big truck, so she drove carefully down the winding gravel road toward the main entrance of the ranch.

She'd never felt this way—hopeful, happy, looking forward to the future. In the last few months her life had been turned upside down. And it was good. The town, the apartment, the jobs at the bar and the vet school, and the people. And, of course, Fisher.

She loved him.

It was a risk, she knew that. But it was a risk she was willing to take. When they were together, she believed everything was going to be okay. Maybe she was fooling herself, but she was going to see this through to the end.

She stopped at the grocery store, picking up a few odds and ends before heading home.

She parked Fisher's truck behind Shots and went into the apartment. She changed, hugging Fisher's shirt close and breathing in his scent again. He'd want it back…but she wasn't going to give it to him until he asked. Instead, she tucked it into a drawer in the dresser.

It was Saturday—laundry day. After Shawn got home, they could go to the Laundromat. She stripped the sheets off the bed, using one of the pillowcases as the laundry bag. Once she'd tossed her clothes inside, she pulled open the closet. As small as it was, she was surprised at the mess inside. She knelt, pulling all the clothes out and tossing them onto the couch. She didn't know what was clean and what was dirty. But as she threw a pair of jeans onto the couch, something slid from the pocket and hit the floor.

She picked it up, turning over the oblong metal case. She lifted the lid. It was some sort of video game. She didn't remember seeing it before. She tucked it aside and pulled the sheets off Shawn's cot. A gold bracelet, two watches and a wallet fell onto the floor.

She knelt, picking up the jewelry. She shouldn't panic, not yet. She pulled everything out of the closet, searched every pair of pants and every pocket, anyplace he might have stashed something. She found a wad of cash in one sock. On the shelf in the closet were his comic books and a sketch pad…and something else.

She carried the cell phone from the closet and sat on the couch. She didn't know which was worse, her disappointment or her anger. She was angry at him, yes, but she was also angry with herself. She should have been paying closer attention to him, watching out for this. He'd been programmed for this. Jesse had taught him that a big score made him a real man.

And no matter how many times she'd tried to undo the damage Jesse had done, she couldn't. Jesse was the cool one, the one everyone liked, the one everyone wanted to be. At least, in their old world. Shawn might like Fisher and the Boones and Stonewall Crossing, but they hadn't been in Stonewall Crossing long enough for those habits to just go away. If she was being honest with herself, she needed to accept that they might not go away without help.

She stared at the phone, touching the screen to see if it was locked. Maybe she could return it to the owner.

But the call list on the phone popped up and she almost dropped the phone.

Shawn had called Jesse? Not once, but several times?

She froze, all too familiar with the cold that seeped into her bones. She was still sitting there when Shawn walked through the door.

"What's wrong?" Shawn asked.

She looked at him, holding up the phone.

He frowned. "That's mine."

"It is?" she asked. "You bought this? You're paying for service?"

"I found it," he said.

"Where?"

"In the men's restroom," he answered.

"Which men's restroom?"

"Why does it matter? If they wanted the phone, they shouldn't have left it lying around." She'd heard those words before—from Jesse.

"And the jewelry? The money?" she asked. "The video game?"

"Eli gave the video game to me," he said. "You can call and ask him."

"I will," she assured him. "What about the jewelry and the money? Shawn, you know this stuff isn't yours. You know it's wrong, it's illegal to take things that don't belong to you."

He shrugged. "You never got worked up about it before."

"I didn't, you're right." She shook her head. "And you know why. We didn't have a choice then. And I let you do things I should never, ever have let you do. I was scared, I guess. He hurt me, Shawn, he tried to hurt you, too. Don't you remember that?" She paused, swallowing the panic that threatened to choke her. "Why would you call him? Do you miss it?"

He stared at her, his face set.

"You've got to talk to me, Shawn," she pleaded. "I thought you were happy here. What about the horses and camp? Fisher and Eli and Cutter?"

"I am." Shawn shrugged. "But it feels wrong. I feel lazy not helping you get money—like you are doing all the work. You work so hard but you don't make much, you know? I wanted to help." There was anger on his face. "Jesse always gave me things to do, to help out."

"Jesse gave you things to do to make *him* money." She stood. "You're twelve. You have every right to enjoy being a kid. I want you to. That's what you're supposed to do. Not this." She held up the phone. "This has to stop." She swallowed, the fear creeping in on her. "Did you tell him where we are?"

Shawn's expression fell then. He nodded.

She sat on the couch, covering her face with her hands. *No. No. This couldn't be happening.* If he was coming to Stonewall Crossing, they had no choice. She couldn't go back. And she couldn't bear to have Jesse here—to have everything good and special about Stonewall Crossing tainted. "Get your things together," she murmured.

"Kylee, no," he argued. "I don't want to go."

"I don't, either, Shawn. But I don't want Jesse to hurt anyone here—to get even with me." Too many awful images filled her mind. She'd let herself care about people here. And put them in danger.

"He just wants us back," Shawn said. "I told him we weren't coming back."

She glanced at Shawn then. "What did he say?"

Shawn shook his head.

"Shawn?"

"He said he'd find us when he wanted to."

She stood. "We're taking all these things back, Shawn. All of them. Including Eli's game."

He nodded. "Are you mad?"

She stared at her little brother. "I'm sad, Shawn. I understand why you did this but…but I can't get you out of trouble with the law or protect you when you break the law. Do you understand? The way we lived was bad, Shawn. You know that, don't you?" She waited for his nod. "If it hadn't been for Jesse…" She shook her head. "I wish I'd gotten you out of there earlier. I wish you didn't know and do and see all of…that. I'm sorry, Shawn, for putting you through that. But you have to know, after being here, that what we did was wrong?"

He nodded. "I'm sorry."

"Hurry up. I want to wash everything before we leave." She filled both pillowcases with clothes.

"But I don't want to go," Shawn repeated.

"I don't, either," Kylee said, blinking back the tears that stung her eyes. "I don't, either." She sniffed, pressing a kiss to her brother's forehead and wishing with all her heart she could erase every wonderful second with Fisher from her mind.

"WHAT'S UP?" FISHER took the phone Hunter offered him.

"Hey, Fisher, have you talked to Kylee recently?" Josie asked.

"Not since this morning," he answered, wiping the sweat from his brow.

"She and Shawn just left. Shawn took a few of Eli's games without Eli knowing it, and Kylee was making him return them."

Fisher sighed. "I'm sure they were both pretty embarrassed."

"They were. I told them it wasn't a big deal but I could tell it was eating Shawn up. It kills me what they've been through." She paused. "It's just, she said they were leaving town and—"

"What?"

"She said something had come up and they had to go. I thought I should tell you since I know, we all know, you care about her," she said.

"Thanks." He thrust the phone at Hunter, his heart pounding a mile a minute. "I need your keys."

Hunter handed them over without question. He could feel the weight of his family's eyes on him but couldn't stop to explain. He had to get to her before she left. Because if she left he knew she'd make it impossible for him to find her.

"We're almost done," Archer called out.

"You'll have to finish without me," he called out, then climbed into Hunter's truck and flew down the road.

What had happened? On the drive from the ranch to town, he sifted through their conversation. She'd said they were on their own—they had no place to go. So why were they leaving now? Was Kylee ashamed because of what Shawn had done? It wasn't right, but it was Shawn's normal. It would probably take some time for Shawn to forget something he'd been trained to do. It was something they'd have to work on.

They. As a team. A family. Because that's what you did when you loved someone. And, dammit, he knew she loved him. Like he loved her. He parked in front of Shots, pushed through the doors, and headed down the hall to the small apartment.

He knocked.

"Hey, Fisher." Shawn opened the door, wearing a hangdog expression.

"Hey, Shawn." Fisher stepped inside, being as calm as possible. The sight of the place, stripped down and cold, turned his stomach to lead. Two large backpacks and one beaten-up suitcase sat packed and on the counter. It was hard to breathe. "Where's Kylee?" He needed to see her, needed to understand what was happening. He'd fix it so they'd never have to leave.

"She's talking to Cutter," he answered.

"You going somewhere?" he asked, panic thickening his tongue.

Shawn nodded.

"Where?" he asked.

The boy shrugged.

"What's going on, Shawn? Things okay?" he didn't mean to interrogate Shawn, but he needed answers—now.

"I messed up," he admitted.

Fisher looked down at Shawn, the hurt and anger in the boy's words begging for Fisher's undivided attention. He drew in a deep breath and laid a hand on the boy's shoulder. "What happened, Shawn? Whatever it is, we can figure this out."

Shawn slowly nodded. "I took some things. Jesse told me the best way to make easy money was to *find* things and sell them to pawnshops. But no one will buy the stuff. I'm too young to sell anything so I've been hiding it all."

Fisher listened carefully, watching the boy's frustration as he spoke.

"I tried to get Jesse to sell it for me, but he wouldn't— said it was my problem." Shawn frowned.

Fisher's blood ran cold. Shawn had talked to Jesse. No wonder Kylee was panicking. "You talked to Jesse? When?"

"Last week." Shawn's eyes filled with tears. "Kylee found the stuff and made me take it all back but she's still upset."

He could understand why Kylee would be upset. It was

a small town and people talked. But that wasn't a solid reason for them to go. But Jesse was—or so Kylee would think. He was the only thing that still scared Kylee. And when she was scared, she ran.

"I've always helped out. I know it was wrong and I feel bad about it but… Kylee's working two jobs and I'm…just drawing and riding horses. It's not fair to her." Shawn's voice broke. "I don't want to go, Fisher."

"Shawn," Kylee said firmly.

He turned, taking in her drawn expression. She looked pale—remote.

"You're the kid. I'm the adult." She brushed past Fisher.

"We don't have to go," Shawn argued.

"We do." Kylee sounded exhausted.

"Why?" Fisher's impatience got the better of him. He hadn't meant to be so loud or gruff, but dammit, there was no way he was going to let them go if he could stop it. "Where are you going and why?"

"Here." She handed him his truck keys, still avoiding his gaze.

He gently took hold of her wrist. "Kylee, look at me. Look at me and tell me what you're thinking. Please."

She shook her head.

Shawn spoke up. "Jesse knows where we are."

"I figured as much." Fisher nodded. "So?"

That made Kylee look at him. "So?"

"Let him come." Fisher slid his hand up her arm and beneath her hair to her neck. "He's not going to hurt you. Not here. I won't let him."

She stared at him, her blue eyes full of pain. She shrugged away from his touch. "I can't do that to you, Fisher. I can't do…*this*. *Any* of this…"

Her words hung in the silence. She was upset. So he

needed to calm her down. "Shawn said he talked to Jesse a week ago." He stood, fighting the urge to reach for her. "He's not going to come after you. He has no power here. It doesn't make sense. You two weren't the only ones working for him, were you? Why come all this way for you two?"

Part of him wished he was wrong—that Jesse would show up. It'd feel good to beat the man senseless…but it wouldn't change the way Shawn or Kylee felt. Or Kylee's urge to run. And, right now, that's what mattered.

She shook her head. "Jesse doesn't do things that make sense. He's unpredictable. And dangerous. If we're gone, he won't stay…"

"Kylee," he whispered. The sound of her name was rough, full of the pain tearing through him.

"I don't want your family—or you—hurt because of my mistakes." She glanced at her brother. "Shawn and I can take care of ourselves."

"Can't we stay, Kylee?" Shawn's voice broke. "I'm sorry. I thought he'd help me." Shawn added, "But he said I wasn't his problem anymore."

"You're not a problem." Kylee hugged Shawn. "You're an amazing young man with a big heart. You're a good person. He's… He is not. Please don't listen to him."

"Kylee's right," Fisher agreed, his mind racing. He looked at Kylee, waiting for her to look at him. When she did, he wasn't expecting to see tears. He reached up, wiping them away. "Don't go." It was a plea and an order. He couldn't make her stay, no matter how much he wanted to. His only choice was to lay it all out there. "You are my family. You and Shawn. I love you both. I'm not going to let you go without a fight."

She shook her head again. "This isn't your fight."

"Maybe I want it to be," he said softly, hoping she'd let him in. Where he belonged.

"You don't understand," she said.

"You're right, I don't. But I want to." His gaze searched hers, giving rise to a glimmer of hope. He needed more time, to help her and Shawn come up with the best possible options.

She stared at him, her blue eyes boring into his. "I want you to go," she said, so softly he thought he'd misheard. She turned away to pick up her backpack. "Come on, Shawn, we need to get out of here." Fisher had never felt such panic.

"But next week…" Shawn stopped, his lips pressed together.

But, even as his heart was breaking, Fisher understood. "Camp." Next week was what Shawn had been waiting for. "Starts Monday—"

"I don't have to go to camp," Shawn said, his voice dull and resigned. He picked up his backpack, sniffing softly. "This is my fault anyway."

"Shawn…" She sat on the couch, covering her face with her hands. "Dammit."

Fisher didn't know what to do. There had to be a way to give them what they wanted—without losing them. But his mind was blank, still processing the last ten minutes and trying to make sense of what had happened. All he could do was be there. "What do you need?" he asked.

Kylee glanced at him, her eyes sparkling with tears. "I've got this, Fisher. We'll be fine. You…you can go."

That was the one thing he couldn't do. Leave her? Shawn? Now? "I can't," he forced the words out.

There was a knock on the door then, startling them all. Fisher saw the way they jumped, how wide-eyed they were as they stared at the door. And it made his blood boil. How could he convince them he'd protect them? How could he explain that he would never let anyone or anything hurt—control them—again?

"Fisher?" It was Renata. "Kylee? Sorry to break up the snuggle fest."

Fisher saw the siblings exchange a look, saw the instant easing of Kylee's posture and expression. Instead of guarded and tense, Kylee looked defeated. And it tore at his heart.

Fisher opened the door to find his sister, smiling broadly, completely unaware that his heart was breaking and his world was falling apart.

"I talked Dad into bowling and thought you three might want to go…" Her voice faded and her smile dimmed. She paused, staring long and hard at him, Kylee and then Shawn. She stepped inside, sliding a reassuring arm around the boy's shoulders. "Looks like you all could use some cheering up. And don't tell me it's nothing or to mind my own business, Fisher, because you know that's not going to happen. What's going on and how do we fix it?"

Chapter Twelve

Fisher stood, watching the wind blow through Kylee's long black hair. Her attention was focused on Shawn riding around the corral. Not that she needed to worry, Shawn had more than proved himself as an able horseman this week. Still, she leaned into the fence, her forehead resting on the top beam, her arms crossed. Fisher could see the lift of her lips as Shawn glanced her way and knew she'd smiled that smile at her little brother.

His heart twisted sharply, the air he breathed in razor sharp and stinging.

Camp was almost over. And nothing had changed.

For four days he'd acted as if all was right with the world. And, according to Renata, he was doing a good job. So what if he'd hung his punching bag on his back porch and pummeled it until his hands were throbbing? No one knew. And it had given him an outlet for the frustration that twisted his insides, at least for a little while. Besides, scowling and stomping around wouldn't do a damn thing to change Kylee's plan to leave.

The problem was, he didn't know what would.

Every day for the last four days, he'd greeted her with a ready smile at work and at the ranch. With Renata and his father's persuasion, Kylee and Shawn had moved all their belongings into one of the rooms at the Lodge. It wasn't far from Stonewall Crossing, but it wasn't where Jesse thought they were. Between Renata and Shawn, Kylee had reluctantly agreed to stay for camp. And that ensured Fisher had more time with them…if only Kylee would cooperate.

Shawn went out of his way to point out how safe the ranch was. While Kylee reminded him over and over that it wasn't their home. Even if that's what Fisher wanted more than anything.

The week was almost up and he'd made no progress.

She dodged every smile or comment he offered, door he held open or hand he offered. Her eyes never met his—unless it was by accident. And then she'd look away, leaving him aching over the pain and sadness in her big blue eyes.

He wasn't giving up. He'd never give up.

"Kylee said yes to Montana," his father said, coming to stand beside him at the fence. "Kind of hard to argue with a job, a roof over your head and the added security of a seventeen-hundred-mile road between here and there."

Fisher nodded. "Makes for a long drive back and forth on date night," he said, smiling.

"Maybe," his father chuckled. "But it was a good call, son. Your aunt Myra's got that place to herself since Tandy and Toben up and left on her. Will do her some good to have extra hands on the farm. And, from the looks of it, Shawn'll get a kick out of that, too."

Fisher nodded again. "Boy looks like he was born on horseback."

"He does at that. He and Trigger have taken a real shine to each other. Maybe it'd help Shawn to have Trigger go with him?" his father asked.

Fisher looked at him.

"Course, you'd have to drive him up in a few weeks, after the camps are done." His father winked at him.

Fisher laughed then. "Never knew you were such a matchmaker, Dad."

"Two down, two to go," his father said. "Gotta keep the family name going and make sure there's enough Boones to keep working the place."

"What if your grandkids are in Montana?" he asked. He'd go, if Kylee asked him to.

"Pretty country up there," his father said. "And it's Boone country, too. Just a might colder in the winter months." His father shivered.

Fisher laughed again. He wasn't a fan of long, cold winters, either. Truth be told, Stonewall Crossing was exactly where he wanted to be. But he'd follow Kylee anywhere if she gave him some inkling that's what she wanted.

He glanced at her only to find those big blue eyes watching him and his father. In unison, he and his father tipped their hats at her. She turned away, but not before he caught a glimpse of her smile. He'd missed that. He missed her.

At the vet school, he lingered at the admissions desk. After work, he headed for the ranch to help Renata—knowing full well Kylee would soon be there. He'd chatted with Shawn, watched the progress the boy had made and tried to engage Kylee when she got there, but she'd shut him down and found a place to stand exactly opposite of him.

"I admire your determination," his father said.

"Some things a man can't give up on," Fisher answered, meaning it. No matter how long it took, he wasn't giving up on Kylee. Or Shawn. He knew they were his family, one he was proud of.

Long after the blue sky turned pink and orange and black, he was still finding things to do in the barn. There were thirty kids in camp so there were thirty horses that needed brushing out, thirty saddles that needed polishing, stalls that needed to be cleaned, plenty of work to wear himself out. When he looked at the clock, it was almost midnight. He wiped his face with his bandanna and started flipping off the extra interior lights.

"It's late." Archer strode into the barn, heading toward the small office. "Why are you here?"

"Helping Renata," Fisher mumbled.

Archer looked pointedly around the empty barn. "Renata?"

Fisher crossed his arms over his chest and stared at his brother. "Why are you here?"

Archer paused, his eyes narrowing slightly as his gaze met Fisher's. "I left my computer cord in the office." He disappeared inside the office briefly. "Have some charts to review before I can power down for the night."

Fisher nodded. He'd caught up on his charts. "Need help?"

Archer shot him a look. "With my charts?"

He nodded.

"It's not like you to mope."

Fisher felt an instant flare of anger. "Mope?"

Archer nodded, pointing. "Mope."

"Anyone ever tell you you're—"

"Opinionated? Honest?"

"An asshole?" Fisher asked.

Archer's eyes went round.

"I accept you're not a people person. I accept that you

don't believe in love because it's not concrete enough for you." Fisher's words were hard. "I can't prove or explain or show it to you but I can tell you it's pretty…damn *great*. And losing it hurts more than…anything. Like getting kicked in the chest by a horse, over and over and over." He paused. "So how about giving me a break?"

"Being kicked repeatedly by a horse would be painful. And it might kill you." Archer's tone was anything but sympathetic.

Fisher sighed long and loud, shaking his head in pure exasperation. "That's about right."

Archer stood there, his computer cord clutched in one white-knuckle fist. He frowned at Fisher, his lips pressed tight as he stepped forward and pulled Fisher into a hard embrace. Fisher was too startled to speak, his brother's uncharacteristic show of affection awkward. And comforting.

KYLEE GLANCED AT the clock. It was two in the morning. Shawn snored in the other double bed, oblivious to her tossing and turning. She'd counted sheep, stared at a single spot on the ceiling and gone through the ways to make various drinks—but nothing helped. She was wide-awake.

Maybe it was because the Lodge was so quiet.

Maybe she was worried about this weekend, their trip—starting over.

She drew in a wavering breath.

She didn't lie. She shouldn't start now. She knew the truth. It was Fisher. Somehow the thought of leaving him scared her more than anything else. Even Jesse. She didn't know what to do. Or how to bear the almost unbearable pain in her chest that thoughts of heading to Montana prompted.

The last few days he'd stood by silently, wanting to help, offering a smile or some word of comfort. And every smile or word of encouragement tugged at her heart, challenging her resolve to hold him at arm's length. She knew it was the right thing to do, for him.

She'd never had something to give up before. Now she was giving up so much. Her job. Her friends—something she'd never had before. A community and friends for Shawn.

And Fisher. And all the love and joy and hope he gave her. It always came back to him. To the aching emptiness that threatened to swallow her whole if she left.

If she stayed…

She slid from her bed and padded across the thick, plush carpet to peer out the glass pane of the French doors. The full moon was bright, spilling into their room and illuminating the Lodge's wide wraparound porch. If Teddy Boone hadn't insisted they stay with him, where would they be now? On the road, probably. Her money wouldn't have run out, but they'd both be jumpy and tired by now. Instead, they were surrounded and protected by acres of Boone land. Shawn was happy—suntanned, exhausted and happy. And she was lonely. Even surrounded by the Boones, she ached for more. She ached for Fisher.

It would be better when they left. When she didn't see him every day…

She closed her eyes, panic and grief washing over her. She wouldn't see him every day. She wouldn't hear his laugh or know that he'd drop everything if she needed him. Leaving him would be the hardest thing she'd ever done. If she could do it.

Staying wasn't an option. If Jesse came…

She pressed her forehead to the cold glass. What if he came? She swallowed, trying to picture Jesse. Here. But she couldn't.

Was Fisher right? Was his threat just a threat? It didn't make sense for him to leave Las Vegas. Why come all this way for two people who would only cause him trouble—the one thing he took pains to avoid? And if he came, what would happen? He'd yell, maybe throw a few punches, but he couldn't force them to go. He wouldn't touch the Boones, he was too smart for that.

So why was she leaving? She swallowed, allowing herself the freedom to think—to hope.

Everything she'd ever wanted, even though she'd had no idea, was right here. She and Shawn had been given a real chance at a real life. With people who loved them. With a man who would always take care of them.

Shawn snorted, rolled over and sighed, making her smile.

Let him come. He's not going to hurt you. Not here. I won't let him. Fisher's words reached her.

She slipped through the French door, sighing as a warm evening breeze blew against the oversize T-shirt she was sleeping in. She walked forward and rested her hip against the railing, listening to the chirp of the cicadas and crickets and the distant hoot of an owl. Out here, the sky was blue black, sparkling with millions of stars in a cloudless sky. Her gaze wandered, until she saw something from the corner of her eye.

Fisher was sprawled in one of the deck chairs, his long legs stretched out in front of him and his cowboy hat tipped forward on his head. One arm dangled off the side of the chair, the other lay across his chest. A soft snore reached her.

She stared at him, her heart thumping while every inch of her demanded she go to him. So she did. She leaned forward, carefully lifting his hat to stare down at him. He was so damn handsome, rough and big and manly and…gorgeous. She loved him.

"Kylee?" His eyes popped open. "You okay? What's wrong?"

She crouched by his chair, taking his hand in hers. "I'm sorry, Fisher."

He blinked, not awake. "For what?"

"For the last four days." She cradled his hand against her chest, loving its warmth and solid feel. "For putting you through…what I've put you through."

He sat forward then, his hand turning to hold on to hers. "No apologies, Kylee. I hurt for what you're going through—"

"And I hurt you by shutting you out," she interrupted.

His green eyes, heavy-lidded as they were, peered into hers.

Her heart was hammering as she searched for the right words. "I know what I want—"

"I know," he said, his hand tightening on hers. "I might not want you to go, but I'll support you. Doesn't mean I'm giving you up, Kylee. If you and Shawn decide there's room for me, I bet Montana could use another vet."

"You'd do that?" she whispered, stunned once more by the love of this man.

He nodded, his gaze sweeping her face.

"You're what I want, Fisher. Here, in Stonewall Crossing." She was instantly pulled into his lap, his heavily muscled arms holding her against his broad chest. "I love you."

"I love you." He stared down at her. "And everything's going to be okay."

She nodded, running her fingers down his cheek. "I know."

The corners of his eyes crinkled as he grinned. "Good."

She tugged his head down to hers, brushing her lips against his. "Thank you."

"For what?" he asked, kissing her again.

"For loving me, as I am. And Shawn." She hesitated. "I want to stay, Fisher, but I worry about Jesse—about putting you and your family at risk."

"If he comes, we'll deal with it. I won't let you down, I promise you. We're strong together. Me, you and Shawn. We're a family, Kylee." Fisher cupped her cheek. "If you want to be..."

"It's all I want. I couldn't leave, Fisher. I can't let you go," she said softly.

Fisher pressed a kiss to her forehead. "Then don't, Kylee. Just hold on to me, love me and know I'm never letting you go."

Epilogue

"All happening so quick, people are gonna think this is a shotgun wedding," Cutter said, patting the hand she'd placed on his arm.

"Maybe it is," she whispered, kissing the old man's cheek. She and Fisher had yet to tell the rest of the family that there would be a new member of the Boone family. Annabeth and Ryder's twins were only a few weeks old and she didn't want to steal their thunder.

Their baby hadn't been planned, but Fisher's unfiltered excitement had chased away her anxiety. Even Shawn was thrilled. He didn't care if it was a boy or a girl, as long as he got to teach them to draw. Listening to the two of them discussing baby names, Fisher's mission to read every maternity book ever written, and how soon was too soon to get the baby a pony made it impossible not to be delighted. And so she was. She was going to be a wife and, in about six months, she was going to be a mother.

"Well, now, we best get a move on then," Cutter smiled. "A baby."

"A secret I'd appreciate you kept—for now," she said, squeezing his hand.

He snorted, leading her out the back doors of the Lodge and down the steps to the large deck. Cutter wasn't the fastest escort but she didn't mind. She needed plenty of time to navigate the stairs without tripping on the hem of her white lace wedding dress or the length of her veil.

She felt like a princess, surrounded by lanterns, candles and thousands of white twinkling lights. Renata had outdone herself, transforming the space into something truly magical. And there, waiting for her, was her Prince Charming.

The look on Fisher's face took her breath away. He loved her. He was proud of her. And he thought she was beautiful. And he let her know it every single day.

Shawn was at his side, the only groomsman. He hadn't liked the idea of giving her away. Instead, he'd wanted to wait for her with Fisher—since the three of them were now a family. It was kind of hard to argue with his logic, so they hadn't.

"You treat her right or I'll hunt you down," Cutter said, placing Kylee's hand in Fisher's.

"I will," Fisher said, chuckling.

All she saw was Fisher. His steady green gaze held hers throughout the ceremony, promising her all the comfort and love she could ever need. His hands were steady, even though she was shaking like a leaf. This big, strong man was hers now—forever. No matter what life might throw their way, he would always be there for them—her, Shawn and their baby.

When it was time, she said the vows, slid the thick gold band onto his finger and tilted her face up for his kiss.

"You look beautiful, Mrs. Boone," he whispered against her lips.

"You make me feel beautiful, Dr. Boone," she said, kissing him again.

When the minister pronounced them Dr. and Mrs.

Boone the guests clapped and Shawn headed off in search of Eli.

Fisher pulled her arm through his, covering her hand. "I could stand here looking at you all night, but I'm thinking our guests might not appreciate that." His gaze swept over her face as his hand came up to cradle her cheek.

"I'm not sure I'd want to stand here all night so you can look at me." She leaned into his touch.

"No?" he asked, cocking an eyebrow. "What do you want me to do instead?"

She smiled, sliding her arms around his neck. "For starters, I want you to kiss me."

"Anytime, Kylee, anytime."

* * * * *

Be sure to look for the next story in
THE BOONES OF TEXAS *series by Sasha Summers,*
available in 2017
wherever Harlequin books and ebooks are sold!

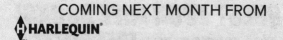

REQUEST YOUR FREE BOOKS!
2 FREE NOVELS PLUS 2 FREE GIFTS!

◆ HARLEQUIN®

~Western ~Romance

ROMANCE THE ALL-AMERICAN WAY!

YES! Please send me 2 FREE Harlequin® Western Romance novels and my 2 FREE gifts (gifts are worth about $10). After receiving them, if I don't wish to receive any more books, I can return the shipping statement marked "cancel." If I don't cancel, I will receive 4 brand-new novels every month and be billed just $4.74 per book in the U.S. or $5.49 per book in Canada. That's a savings of at least 12% off the cover price! It's quite a bargain! Shipping and handling is just 50¢ per book in the U.S. and 75¢ per book in Canada.* I understand that accepting the 2 free books and gifts places me under no obligation to buy anything. I can always return a shipment and cancel at any time. Even if I never buy another book, the two free books and gifts are mine to keep forever.

154/354 HDN GJ5V

Name _____ (PLEASE PRINT) _____

Address _____ Apt. # _____

City _____ State/Prov. _____ Zip/Postal Code _____

Signature (if under 18, a parent or guardian must sign) _____

Mail to the **Reader Service:**
IN U.S.A.: P.O. Box 1867, Buffalo, NY 14240-1867
IN CANADA: P.O. Box 609, Fort Erie, Ontario L2A 5X3

Want to try two free books from another line?
Call 1-800-873-8635 or visit www.ReaderService.com.

* Terms and prices subject to change without notice. Prices do not include applicable taxes. Sales tax applicable in N.Y. Canadian residents will be charged applicable taxes. Offer not valid in Quebec. This offer is limited to one order per household. Not valid for current subscribers to Harlequin Western Romance books. All orders subject to credit approval. Credit or debit balances in a customer's account(s) may be offset by any other outstanding balance owed by or to the customer. Please allow 4 to 6 weeks for delivery. Offer available while quantities last.

Your Privacy—The Reader Service is committed to protecting your privacy. Our Privacy Policy is available online at www.ReaderService.com or upon request from the Reader Service.

We make a portion of our mailing list available to reputable third parties that offer products we believe may interest you. If you prefer that we not exchange your name with third parties, or if you wish to clarify or modify your communication preferences, please visit us at www.ReaderService.com/consumerchoice or write to us at Reader Service Preference Service, P.O. Box 9062, Buffalo, NY 14240-9062. Include your complete name and address.

SPECIAL EXCERPT FROM

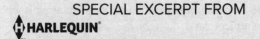

HARLEQUIN®

Western Romance

*The minute he recovers from injury, Trace Delaney
will get back to bull riding, pick up and move on as
he always does. But can Annie Owen and her twin
daughters change his mind?*

Read on for a sneak preview of
THE BULL RIDER'S HOMECOMING,
the second book in Jeannie Watt's
MONTANA BULL RIDERS *miniseries.*

The girls were waiting at the top of the stairs when Annie opened the cellar door. They high-fived their mom, and Trace grinned as they went to stand on the heater vents when the furnace began to blow.

"No more dollar eating," Katie announced.

"Just the normal amount of dollar eating," Annie corrected before shooting a look Trace's way.

Dismissed?

"Well...those chores are waiting," he said.

"We can play a game next time you come by," Kristen assured him.

Trace crouched down in front of her, feeling only a little awkward as he said, "I look forward to that. And it was a lot of fun riding with you guys today."

"We're not guys. We're girls," Kristen informed him.

"I stand corrected," Trace said as he got to his feet. Tough crowd.

"I'll walk you to your truck," Annie said.

Escorted from the premises. So much for that whisper of disappointment he'd thought he saw cross her face. Maybe he was the one who was disappointed. But he'd promised to leave as soon as the furnace was fixed, and he was a man of his word.

Annie slipped into her coat and followed Trace out of the house. The air was still brisk from the storm, but the setting sun cast warm golden light over Annie's neatly kept yard. Everything about her place was warm and homey, the exact opposite of what he knew when he'd been growing up. He hoped the twins would look back in the years ahead and appreciate the home their mother had made for them.

Trace stopped before opening his truck door and looked down at Annie, who was wearing a cool expression. The woman was hard to read. On the one hand, he thought maybe she liked him. On the other, she couldn't hurry him out of there fast enough.

"Thanks again," she said.

"Anytime." One corner of his mouth quirked up before he said, "I mean that, you know."

Annie's lips compressed and she nodded, then she raised her hand and brushed her fingers against his cheek, just as he'd done to her earlier. He felt his breath catch at the light touch. Then he captured her hand with his and leaned down to take her lips in a kiss that surprised both of them.

Don't miss
THE BULL RIDER'S HOMECOMING
by Jeannie Watt, available September 2016 wherever
Harlequin® Western Romance
books and ebooks are sold.

www.Harlequin.com

Wrangle Your Friends for the Ultimate Ranch Girls' Getaway

Win an all-expenses-paid 3-night luxurious stay for you and your 3 guests at The Resort at Paws Up in Greenough, Montana.

Retail Value $10,000

A TOAST TO FRIENDSHIP, AN ADVENTURE OF A LIFETIME!

Learn more at
www.Harlequinranchgetaway.com

Sweepstakes ends August 31, 2016

WCHMR

HARLEQUIN®

A *Romance* FOR EVERY MOOD™

JUST CAN'T GET ENOUGH?

Join our social communities
and talk to us online.

You will have access to the latest
news on upcoming titles and special
promotions, but most importantly,
you can talk to other fans about your
favorite Harlequin reads.

Harlequin.com/Community

 Facebook.com/HarlequinBooks

 Twitter.com/HarlequinBooks

Pinterest.com/HarlequinBooks